A MAN WHO HA
AND THE WOM
QUESTIO

C. S. Lewis was a man of the mind, and his mind
had served him well. His writings had won him fame
and fortune. His bookish knowledge and bone-dry
wit shone brilliantly in the sheltered atmosphere of
Oxford University where scholars were treated like
royalty, and C. S. Lewis was freed of all worldly
cares.

Then into this Eden of the intellect came Joy
Gresham, with her New York accent, her unfettered
tongue, her most American cast of thought, and own
special mode of showing her feelings and acting
on them.

You might say that C. S. Lewis was too old for love.
You might say that he was too sensible for love.
You might say that he was too settled in his ways to
have his life, his views, his everything, turned inside
out and upside down.

You would be wrong.

SHADOWLANDS

SHADOWLANDS

A NOVEL BY
Leonore Fleischer

BASED ON THE SCREENPLAY BY
William Nicholson
BASED ON HIS STAGEPLAY

Ø

A SIGNET BOOK

SIGNET
Published by the Penguin Group
Penguin Books USA Inc., 375 Hudson Street,
New York, New York 10014, U.S.A.
Penguin Books Ltd, 27 Wrights Lane,
London W8 5TZ, England
Penguin Books Australia Ltd, Ringwood,
Victoria, Australia
Penguin Books Canada Ltd, 10 Alcorn Avenue,
Toronto, Ontario, Canada M4V 3B2
Penguin Books (N.Z.) Ltd, 182–190 Wairau Road,
Auckland 10, New Zealand

Penguin Books Ltd, Registered Offices:
Harmondsworth, Middlesex, England

First published by Signet, an imprint of Dutton Signet, a division of
Penguin Books USA Inc.

First Printing, December, 1993
10 9 8 7 6 5 4 3

 REGISTERED TRADEMARK—MARCA REGISTRADA

Printed in the United States of America

BOOKS ARE AVAILABLE AT QUANTITY DISCOUNTS WHEN
USED TO PROMOTE PRODUCTS OR SERVICES. FOR INFOR-
MATION PLEASE WRITE TO PREMIUM MARKETING DIVI-
SION, PENGUIN BOOKS USA INC., 375 HUDSON STREET, NEW
YORK, NEW YORK 10014.

Contents

Contents

SHADOWLANDS

What's Prologue Is Past

This is the story—not an untrue one, as it happens—of a man who found himself overtaken by surprise long past the usual age of surprises, a man whose heart was compelled to undergo a dramatic change at a time when he thought he was beyond change, a man whose most cherished beliefs were challenged and nearly overwhelmed; a man who, having passed through agonizing fire, discovered a wholly different sort of happiness in the most unlikely way, in the most unexpected place, and at the hands of an extraordinary person so different from himself that, had you informed him in advance, clearly and in detail, of exactly what was about to befall him he would have laughed you off as foolish or loony or both.

For, after all, this is a man who, well advanced along the twisted pathway of life, had never been in love. The flesh interested him very little; it was the life of the mind he'd sought and achieved. This man long inhabited a world of ideas, not emotions, and the ideas in which he believed gave him comfort. He had already achieved what he believed to be an almost perfect happiness, and was convinced that he needed nothing he didn't already possess.

What should a man need to make him happy? First, you must attempt to define the word "happiness," because that most subjectively elusive of nouns is, perhaps, next only to "love" in its slippery variance from one case to the next.

For one man, happiness may mean taking great risks and overcoming unimaginable dangers—scaling Everest, or jumping from an airplane at ten thousand feet. For another, happiness can always be found by his own fireside, with a loving family and a well-stocked pantry, and enough golden-years retirement money in bank certificates and mutual funds. A third man may discover his happiness by bamboozling other men and concluding a deal that puts a few more obscene millions into his numbered Swiss account. A fourth man wants racy cars and desirable women, flashy clothing, fame, a hit record, the adulation of the world. These are perhaps simple forms of happiness, depending on the rush of adrenalin, or constant affection and the peace of mind that comes with security, or hungry greed, or the desire for success and the envy of others, yet they are not unfamiliar forms of triumphant attainment or even unworthy goals. We certainly recognize all of them; our society sanctions and even applauds them. But they are—after all—simple desires.

What of the truly moral and intellectually complex man, for whom happiness cannot be defined, but merely delineated by a number of difficult, labyrinthine, and interdependent factors? What if he's one of those who know that happiness at best is transitory, even ephemeral in nature? He is aware that, on the same morning that the multimillionaire rises depressed and miserable in his penthouse to greet the day, the blind beggar may wake up in his cardboard box laughing out loud in a rush of joy. How does anyone explain that? And, further, how may you grasp at that joy in living and hold it close so that it can't wriggle free? What form of happiness if any can be tamed and made to stick around?

What if a man has never felt the need of another's arms around him, holding him close to give him comfort, has never missed the sound of a child's voice and a woman's singing? Suppose he lives for many years without the agonies and ecstasies of physical love, lives until his heart seems to have shriveled up like a raisin. If a sudden, unexpected flood of emotion, of desperate caring for

3

another, should overtake him unawares, would that poor dried-up little heart burst asunder in one mighty explosion?

But let's return to the special man whose story this is. If anybody has a reason to be truly happy, this man does. He is easy in his skin, a man who has everything he wants out of life, and nothing he doesn't want. He lives, if not in luxury, at least in mental, spiritual and physical comfort. He thinks of himself as a pretty good chap, and with reason. There's no malice in him, and his quiet works of charity are performed as a true Christian performs them, in the hope of Heaven and without expectation of human recognition or reward. Possessing not only morals but ethics as well, he lives his life according to his apprehension of what is the right thing to do. And he's thought long and hard about what is the right thing to do.

Our man is a man respected and admired, not only in his friendly society of peers, but in the world outside his windows. He finds satisfaction and delight in his chosen work, at which he excels. His work is well reviewed, honored and praised; it earns him an excellent living, and he can't even spend all he earns. He's in the physical and mental prime of his life; his health is good, his temper excellent, and he has most of his own teeth and almost all of his own hair. His close companions are congenial and collegial, worth talking to and listening to.

Best of all, he is on excellent terms with God. There is no quarrel between him and the All-Mighty; about the strange way things work out a lot of the time this man may ask his Maker why? but he's pretty secure with his answers. He has even talked about God's mercy on the wireless, and published the answers to man's perplexing questions in a series of intriguing and entertaining treatises about the nature of evil in its struggle with good, and the nature of God's relationship with the human race. His treatises also tackle with impunity such knotty problems as why people must endure pain, why the innocent are made to suffer and the guilty go so frequently unpunished. These little books, with their everyday analogies, are accessible and fun, somewhat like the cryptic crossword puzzles in the London *Times*.

Yet he knows that his Redeemer liveth and he is secure in the love of God and his own eventual redemption and resurrection. This man believes in heaven, and to him, who early in his life did *not* believe but wandered in the black maze of the unsaved soul, this bright light of personal salvation is the greatest happiness of any possible earthly happiness. He praises it often, in the books he writes and the lectures he gives. He writes that this earthly life of ours is but a pale precursor of the blessed life to come, a shadowland, if you will. The best is definitely yet to be, and we will meet it in the eternal hereafter.

Did we forget love? No, no, there is great love in this man's life. His form of Christianity is a youthful, ardent religion, filled with mystical incense-scented ceremonies in which the soul unites with its Creator—the body and the blood of Christ are actually consumed by the worshiper and become a part of him. For this man, there are three forms of love—*Charis,* which is the divine grace that is the root of the word "charity"; Agape, the Christian feast of prayer and Scripture, also defined as the love of God for humankind. In these two, he believes, and he is steeped in their precepts like a teabag in a cup. But the third love, Eros, Greek god of love, is the destroyer, the mischievous shooter of the arrows of lust, who, in the words of blind Homer, "loosens the limbs and damages the mind." Of these three, this man has chosen to experience only two. He has rejected the mischievous god Eros as unworthy, greatly inferior to Charis and Agape. And way, way too messy and inconvenient.

When he himself was an atheist, a young pagan, benighted in his disbelief, not yet the happy Christian he later became, this man was a follower of pagan authors. Reveling in the ancient tongues of Greek and Latin, in which he became expert as a university student of what Americans call "the classics" and the British term "Greats," he devoured the plays of Aeschylos and Euripides and their interpretations of Eros, studying the frantic fervor that carried King Agamemnon to his death at the hands of his wife Clytemnestra and her lover Aegisthos, the carnal jealousy which so consumed the barbarian queen Medea that she willingly carved her own children into gobbets of bloody flesh as revenge upon the philandering husband who left her for a younger, prettier woman.

In Virgil's immortal lines this man wept over abandoned Dido's painful lament for the treacherous Aeneas, contemplated with astonishment the depth of the passion that Paris felt for Helen, a lust which brought down the ancient citadel of Troy. He shuddered as King Oedipus tore out the eyes which had looked so sinfully upon his own mother Jocasta, his willing bed partner. No question about it; that god-youth Eros was a sly dog with a wide streak of meanness and a wicked sense of irony. So, after an unspecified number of exploratory amorous embraces experienced in his youth, pleasant enough yet on the whole time-consuming and troublesome, this man made up his mind: better by far to keep out of the way of Eros's arrows. Love was not for him, period. Shunning Aphrodite, he worshiped instead at the altar of the chaste Athene. So, amazingly, this man had reached the age of fifty-four with an untroubled mind and an unbroken heart.

His religious conversion from heathen to Christian, from the gods of Olympus to the God of Abraham and Peter, was long, reluctant and attained only through agony.

In his own words, "I gave in, and admitted that God was God, and knelt and prayed; perhaps, that night, the most dejected and reluctant convert in all England . . . a prodigal who is brought in kicking, struggling, resentful, and darting his eyes in every direction for a chance of escape."

As little more than a boy himself, fighting in the so-called "war to end all wars" which we now call World War I to differentiate it from all the other world wars, this man saw his best friend killed. He witnessed the painful dyings and maimings of hundreds of shining young men from his university, boys who should have been taking tutorials in book-lined studies or rowing with the Blues or lying on the emerald grass of Oxford's quads, with their heads on the soft laps of the dainty young girls whom they should in normal times be marrying.

Instead, an entire generation of young, brave and terrified men—poets and plumbers, miners and millionaires—died without apparent meaning, their youthful bodies rotting in trenches or lying on open fields as carrion for the ravens, or strung like bloody beads on the barbed wire that separated enemy from enemy. Agonizing not only over Paddy's death but over his own survival, this man began to demand answers from God.

"Why," he asked weeping, "if a good God made the world, why has it gone wrong?"

The more he questioned, the more his belief system developed until, much later, he came to that time when he actually believed that God Himself had entered into the dialogue and was personally giving him the answers he was seeking.

And these answers he wrote down with style and wit and published in his allegorical books, which were easy to read, became popular and profitable, and made him wealthy and famous and very sought after as a radio personality and on the church-lady lecture circuit.

Later, this man's children's fantasy novels would become classics, loved by boys and girls and their parents all over the world, quoted and praised and profitable. They would make him a celebrity.

Oh, he is a lucky, wonderful, good, moral, clever, even brilliant and altogether enviable human being, this man. Smug, perhaps, and maybe a shade too pleased with himself. A bit lofty and detached from the daily grind, certainly, a little too publicly pious for some tastes, but never mind. All that is about to change, swiftly, forcefully, and forever. Keep your eye on him; he's about to be rocked to the depths of his being by an earthquake of emotion. He will never be the same man again. The stuffings will be knocked out of him; he will be flensed raw and turned inside out. And then this man's pain will be terrible to behold.

O N E

The Dreaming Spires

"*B*enedictus *benedicat per Jesum Christum Dominum Nostrum. Amen*," intoned the president.

"Amen," came the response, but the multitude of answering voices was lost in the shuffle of chairs, the harsh rattle of benches, and the clanging of silverware in the long dining hall of Magdalen College, Oxford. Grace having been said, the hungry students settled down in the shadow of the dons' high table to their evening meal in a hubbub of noisy conversation. Only men's voices were heard; the chatter of the undergraduates on the benches, the drone of the dons at the high table, the subtle murmurs of the waiters as they set down the silver-covered dishes of food on the polished wooden table.

Jack Lewis, lost in the words of the Grace, sighed a little, as he always did after Latin prayer. It was an unconscious sound, an automatic response, no doubt the product of years of Latin study, a scholar's appreciation of the beautiful ancient tongue. No doubt, too, the effect of another moment shared with God. He shook off the reverie, and, breaking a small piece off the hard roll on his bread plate, he buttered it thinly— butter still being rationed in austere England in 1952—and took a bite.

Down the line of gowned Oxford dons sitting at the high table went Barker the wine steward, walking slowly, hampered not only by age, but by the heavy tray of wine carafes, one for each diner. The dons had ordered in advance which wine they'd be having with their evening meal, and underneath each flagon on the tray was a scrap of paper with the professor's name and the name and year of the chosen vintage. Every small decanter held about half a bottle of wine.

As Barker, with a shaky hand, set each carafe down on the table before each don, one of them would seize it impatiently, pour out a glass, and take a suspicious sip, to make sure that the college servants had got it right.

"I ordered the '45," muttered Desmond Arding, rolling the wine over his palate, convinced that this could not be the '45.

"Can't beat a bouncy young Beaujolais," Bob

Chafer remarked cheerfully, swallowing a hearty mouthful.

His tray now empty, Barker turned to go. All the diners except one had his carafe. The only one without wine was Major Warren ("Warnie") Lewis, Jack Lewis's elder brother and his guest tonight at the college. His head in the clouds while preparing a lecture, Jack had simply forgotten to order Warnie's chosen vintage. To anyone else, this might seem an oversight, but to the stricken Warnie, watching the retreating wine steward's back, it was a calamity of the highest order. Major Lewis was a man to whom a bottle of something was a necessity of life, second only to oxygen.

Warnie squirmed in his chair, turning to look across the long heavy wooden dining table to where his brother was sitting, surrounded by his fellow dons. "Er, . . . Jack . . . I don't seem to . . ."

But C. S. Lewis, called "Jack" by his fellow scholars and everyone else who knew him well, was too far away to hear Warnie's distress call, so Major Warnie was going drinkless. Tonight Jack Lewis was in his element, and enjoying every minute of it. He loved Oxford, he loved Magdalen College, where as Clive Staples Lewis, elected fellow, he taught the allegorical medieval love poetry, *amour courtois*, idealistic yet chaste, that was so dear to

13

his scholarly heart and upon which he was so expert.

Lewis loved sitting at the high table, several yards long and polished to a high gleam, with its friendly mingling of tradition and grilled trout, of gowned dons exhibiting their superiority over the fresh-faced undergraduates sitting on the benches below. And conversation here, even at its worst, was always stimulating, making up for the frequently overcooked and mediocre food, its emphasis on starches, or "stodge."

"Jack, what a surprise," began Christopher Riley, a good friend and a most worthy opponent in a debate. Christopher, an unbeliever, suffered from existential angst and dearly loved communicating it to others. Especially, he enjoyed provoking C. S. Lewis, whose common-man approach to theology annoyed him, although it was most likely the success of the approach, and its considerable financial rewards that irritated Riley most.

"How so, Christopher?"

"Not out plying your trade?"

Warnie turned to Desmond Arding in his desperation, eyeing couldn't—?" he begged tentatively. His finger pushed his empty wineglass an inch or two in Arding's direction.

But Arding either didn't hear or pretended not to. He took another sip of his wine and made a sour face. "This isn't the '45! I'd take an oath on it!"

"What trade is that, Christopher?" asked Jack Lewis, a small smile playing around the corners of his lips. His bright blue eyes gleamed in anticipation. He knew very well what Riley was referring to, and he smelled a dialogue in the wind, an argument between believer and agnostic.

"I see you as a species of medieval peddler, selling relics of the saints. Of dubious authenticity," Riley added wickedly.

Oh, good, it was to be Lewis's fervent and well-paying Christianity on the firing line tonight. If there was anything C. S. Lewis enjoyed, it was his role as Defender of the Faith, the Apostle to the Skeptics. It was the precise sort of argument Lewis most relished. *Credo quia impossibile*. The defense of the rational, natural moral order of the universe.

Uptable, Warnie was parched; he could hardly endure the sight of all those doddering scholars swilling down fine wines while a forgotten military hero went thirsty. Seeing no help forthcoming from Desmond Arding, he gave up and turned to another quarter.

"Claude?" he pleaded.

But Claude Bird was well into his eighties; he was too old and too deaf—even with the bulky hearing aid he wore—to hear Warnie's plaintive mew for help.

The Reverend "Harry" Harrington, Chaplain of Magdalen College, and therefore as enthusiastic a Christian as Jack, stepped in and took up the cudgels in Jack Lewis's defense. "Fair play, Christopher," he protested mildly. "Jack's no Roman, you know."

Riley waved one manicured hand loftily, and the broad sleeve of his black academic gown flapped like the wing of a rook. "I speak metaphorically, Harry. Jack's trade is the manufacture and supply of easy answers to difficult questions."

It was a good shot and right on target; a deep chuckle went up from those within earshot. C. S. Lewis's Christianity-for-the-Workingman bestsellers were small cockleburs in the hides of some of his more envious colleagues. They resented the fact that Lewis's well-received radio lectures on faith and moral behavior had made him something of a celebrity outside the academic realm. Moreover, two years ago, Lewis had released a children's book, a Christian-allegory fantasy novel set in a magical land called Narnia. *The Lion, the Witch and the Wardrobe* increased his fame and his bank account enormously, to the chagrin of some of the other dons. Reviewed as an instant classic, *The Lion* was to be only the first in the ongoing series

The Chronicles of Narnia, which would eventually comprise seven phenomenally successful volumes.

The laughter made Claude Bird uncomfortable. His deafness caused him to always miss jokes, and he hated that. He turned to young Bob Chafer. "What's he say?"

"Rupert?" pleaded Warnie, at the end of his tether. Surely *somebody* ought to offer the college's dinner guest a drink. But Rupert Parrish's thoughts were not on wine, but on *The Lion, the Witch and the Wardrobe, Prince Caspian: The Return to Narnia,* and *The Voyage of the "Dawn Treader,"* Lewis's children's fantasy novels.

"Warnie, I've been meaning to ask you. About your brother's books—does he actually know any children?"

"Children? Jack? I don't think so," answered Warnie Lewis distractedly. His plight seemed more and more hopeless. He was perishing for a drink here, and all Parrish could talk about was his brother and children. Once more, he began to send signals down the dining table to Jack.

"How on earth does he pull it off?" wondered Parrish out loud.

Arding signaled to the wine steward, who was approaching with a tray on which rested a single carafe of wine. "This is not the Chambertin '45, Barker," he scowled.

"To the best of my belief it is, sir. Just a moment, sir." He set the carafe down carefully at Warnie's right hand, but Warnie, still intent on signaling his brother, didn't notice.

Now Rupert Parrish called down the table to Lewis. "I'm intrigued, Jack. Apparently you don't know any actual children—"

Lewis exploded into laughter. "Balderdash. Who says I don't know any children?" he demanded.

"Warnie."

Jack looked at his brother, who, catching his eye, touched his empty glass and turned it over sadly. Jack smiled; when he'd noticed that Barker had missed Warnie, he'd realized his oversight and ordered an excellent claret immediately. Now he pointed to Warnie's right elbow, where the wine, red as heart's blood, appeared as though by magic. Seeing Warnie happy made Jack smile, and he turned his attention back to his colleague Parrish.

"My brother was a child once, Rupert. And, unlikely as it may seem, so was I."

A fair shot across Parrish's bow, but it only served to start up a babble of argument down the table, with Christopher Riley leading the attack and only Lewis and the Reverend Harrington for the defense. The debate became lively, and lasted through coffee and port, and had not concluded when the chairs were pushed back as a signal that the evening meal had come to an end.

Although these were all Oxford dons—from the Latin word "*dominus*" meaning master or teacher— they were not all equally accomplished or gifted with equal intelligence. Several of them were not so much scholars as scholiasts, those diligent book- worms who are content to dot the "i's" of history with little critical markings, adding a footnote here and an asterisk there, debating the particle "*en*" in Attic Greek, or the subtle meanings of the Latin "*et*" as in "*Timeo Danaos et dona ferentes.*"

For these professors, the university tower was not only ivory, it was ivory-lined with goosedown, so successful was their isolation from worldly struggles. Even the younger dons, who had in 1939 and 1940 ventured out into a world gone mad and fought bravely in the war, had now retreated back to the familiar comforts of the library and the chapel, morning tea, and afternoon sherry, town and gown, the pub for a pint and a pork pie, the sound of crystalline voices rising at evensong in chapel, pleasant strolls in Oxford's famous gar- dens. Most of them lived in a cloistered atmosphere of their own architecture, where they could pursue their precious studies and every now and again emerge to publish a scholarly paper or even a book. It was a world that for the most part had no room for women, apart from the occasional drab brown wren of a wife. Women stayed in the kitchen making tea, while the men solved the philosophical problems of the universe, or divined the exact meaning of a tricky phrase of Catullus's.

Even for C. S. Lewis, who had only one foot in Oxford and the other out in the real world, there were no women. The cloistered part of his existence was fashioned around the Trinity of Christianity, his writings, and his love of medieval literature and courtly love poetry, the chastity of which tied in so neatly with his own reliance on Agape, not Eros. His lectures were popular and always well attended, and delivered to an enthusiastic reception. As for his students, they were, if not always cream, then surely the top milk out of the bottle, and Lewis expected great things from them.

At the hour when Jack and Warnie Lewis left Magdalen and started up High Street, the ringing of Great Tom, the sonorous bell in Christ Church Tower, was ringing, so it must be just after nine in the evening, because at nine-oh-five every night Tom tolled one hundred and one times, an Oxford tradition. The tradition dated back centuries, to when one hundred and one students were enrolled in Christ Church College, and each of them was called back home individually by the tolling of a bell. It was a cold night in early autumn, and very clear. Both men wore overcoats and hats, woolen mufflers, and gloves.

"Going to be a frost tonight," remarked Jack, glancing up at the sky, which was illuminated by a splendid show of the constellations.

Warnie looked up at the heavens, tottering a little. He'd finished every drop of his wine and several glasses of after-dinner port, and now he was drunk. "Too many stars. It confuses me."

The brothers walked quietly together, in perfect harmony, only occasionally breaking their silence. After so many years of living together, as boys and as men—all their lives, really, except for the war in which both had served—they understood each other too well to need many words. From time to time, Warnie would straggle off the path in a fog of alcohol, but Jack would grasp his elbow firmly and with fondness, bringing him back again. This walk from the college up Headington Hill to The Kilns was one they had taken at least several thousand times. Behind them, as the hill rose gently, lay the lights of Oxford and the Gothic stone spires of the chapels and colleges, like human fingers reaching out for heaven.

In 1930, Jack had bought The Kilns, a comfortable old house a mile or so outside Oxford. It was built around 1900 and boasted eight acres of wonderful gardens and even a woodland containing a small lake. A pair of disused pottery kilns came with the property, but were now overgrown by vines in a picturesque way.

Jack and Warnie Lewis had lived there now for twenty-two years, close brothers and even closer friends, moving peacefully if not intimately together into middle age. They had no cat or dog, which is rare for the British, who are so passionate about animals. But they didn't feel the need for the company of lower creatures, or for their affection and loyalty. They had each other; they had unbroken peace and quietude; what more did they need?

The house was sizable enough for all their needs, including the need for privacy. There was a large study which they shared on the ground floor, where both of them did their writing, each at his own desk, each at his own work, neither infringing upon the other. The study was the heart of the house, a comfortable if shabby book-lined room that smelled of stale pipe smoke. It was there they took their morning coffee and it was usually there they took their afternoon tea. Mrs. Young, a plump and taciturn housekeeper, looked after all their domestic needs.

Warnie was writing a history of the court of the French king Louis XIV, a long and slow work.

Jack's desk was set at right angles to Warnie's, facing the crowded bookcases and the comfortable easy chairs. One of his quiet joys was the sight of a pool of golden lamplight spreading over his papers, and the feeling of being shut in with his work and his thoughts.

Speaking of his work . . . "The week's almost gone," Jack said, "and I haven't done half my letters."

"You don't—" began Warnie, but Jack finished the sentence for him.

"—have to write back. I know."

"It only encourages them." Warnie didn't understand why his brother felt he had to take the time to answer every letter from every reader who borrowed a C. S. Lewis book from the lending library.

"Yes, yes, yes," smiled Jack. It was a duty imposed on him only by himself; these people, having read his words in covers, felt they knew him and had the right to his personal time, and who was he to say no to them? A polite response, a few encouraging yet impersonal words, a twopenny stamp—it didn't add up to very much.

The cool air of Headington Hill was beginning to dissipate the mist of wine clouding Warnie's brain. He whacked with his stick at a broken branch which had fallen into the path. " 'Mr. C. S. Lewis thanks you for your letter, but he has nothing whatever to say in reply,' " he suggested with a smile. Jack couldn't help chuckling in appreciation of the modest jest. There was more than a germ of truth in it. His replies to his readers were invariably cordial but noncommittal. He rarely heard from the same stranger twice.

By now the two men had reached the path that led to the unlocked front door of The Kilns. With Warnie in front, they went up the path single file. At the door, his brother went in, but Jack turned to catch one more glimpse of the heavens, with its round yellow moon and millions upon uncounted millions of scintillating stars. Surely the stars were God's masterpieces, second only to humankind. He felt a gentle thrill go through him at the majestic sight, and he took in a deep breath of the night air. Now it was time to go inside.

In the hallway, Warnie was switching on lights. Since the house had no central heating, both men kept their coats on, although they hung their hats and mufflers on pegs in the entryway. Warnie headed for the kitchen.

"Nightcap?" he called over his shoulder.

"No, I don't think so," said Jack, who never drank very much, not out of any moralistic disapproval, but because he wanted always to be in control of himself, and liked to have his wits about him. He went now into his study, where he opened his thick desk diary and ran his finger down the lists of tomorrow's appointments. He also looked at the pile of letters waiting for his answers, and sighed. Every hour of the next day was filled. Perhaps he'd answer them the day after tomorrow. Of all God's precious gifts, time was the one that was never given with a lavish hand.

Going back out into the hall, Jack met Warnie at the foot of the staircase. His brother was carrying two hot water bottles, one of which he handed to Jack, and a large tumbler of whiskey. Warnie would sleep soundly tonight.

"London tomorrow," said Jack as they climbed the stairs.

"Disabled veterans? Church widows?" teased Warnie.

The renowned author C. S. Lewis was invited to speak everywhere. He rarely refused, not because of the fees he was paid, but because it gave him a chance to evangelize, to discourse on his chosen subject of God and man, to see men and women sit up and pay fresh attention to a subject they had usually taken for granted. Lewis wanted his listeners to actively think about God's grace, and to rejoice in it as he did himself.

"Association of Christian Teachers."

Now they had reached the upper landing, and

parted, as they had done for so many years, each into his solitary bachelor's bedroom.

" 'Night, Jack."

" 'Night, Warnie."

And, as they had virtually every night for twenty-two years, the two bedroom doors closed at the same time.

Jack was right; last night had brought a touch of frost. The paved path from the front door was covered in gelid moisture. The morning was chilly and damp, with a gray sky through which a weak autumnal sun struggled to cast a few pale rays.

"Morning, Paxford," said Lewis to his gardener as he stepped briskly out of the house to get to his morning seminar at college. He was carrying a battered leather briefcase filled with books and papers.

"Mr. Jack," acknowledged the shriveled old gardener, chopping away at the hedges with a huge pair of clippers.

"Do we want more rain or don't we?"

Paxford shrugged his bony shoulders. "Makes no odds. If we get rain, it'll bring out the mildew on the roses. If we don't, the spring cabbages'll die."

Without breaking stride, Jack Lewis gave this conundrum the serious consideration it merited.

"Alternatively, if it rains, good for the cabbages, and if it doesn't, good for the roses."

Paxford nodded gloomily. "I'm not one to set myself up for falling down, Mr. Jack."

"Nor you are, Paxford, nor you are."

On the walk down the hill to Magdalen College, C. S. Lewis contemplated the hard choices life so often presents—cabbages or roses? The problem of the useful but unlovely versus the beautiful but inedible. For Lewis, there was only one choice— the rose. Take care of the rose and the cabbage would take care of itself.

"A garden, enclosed by a high wall. Inside the garden, a fountain. In the fountain, two crystal stones." Jack's bright blue eyes sent forth beams of sapphire light as he warmed to his subject. When he spoke, in the magic spell cast by his cultured voice and the gestures of his fine hands one could almost see the enchanted walled garden he was describing.

"In the crystals, in reflection, a rose garden. In the midst of the roses, one perfect rosebud. Guillaume de Lorris is using the rosebud as an image, of course. But an image of what?" Lewis threw the challenge out into the room, his voice reverberating with drama.

A handful of youthful faces looked back into

his—the undergraduates who were reading the allegorical *Romance of the Rose* in C. S. Lewis's lectures on courtly poetry. Professor Lewis himself was the acclaimed author of a standard work on the subject, *The Allegory of Love: A Study in Medieval Tradition*, which was, of course, required reading for this term.

"Love?" suggested Montrose Frith, who was usually the first to answer.

"Love," nodded Lewis. "But what kind of love?"

"Untouched? Unopened? Like a bud?" Davydd Standish's brow wrinkled as he voiced the concept.

"Yes. More."

"Perfect love?" asked Frith tentatively.

"What makes it perfect?" Lewis demanded.

"Is it the courtly ideal of love?" asked Alexander Edward Paul Lieven slowly.

"Yes, but what's that? What's its one essential quality?" C. S. Lewis looked around the book-lined room at his students, daring them to think, to envisage, to dream the courtly dream, to immerse themselves in the rich and complex meanings of the poetry. His fondest hope was that he could get through to his students, to get them to unravel the puzzle of life, to make an impact on their thinking about life and love.

The young men sat silent, staring back at their

don, waiting for him to tell them. And he did so, with a flair that was almost theatrical.

"Unattainability. The most intense joy lies not in the having, but in the *desiring*. The delight that never fades, the bliss that is eternal, is only yours when what you most desire is just out of your reach. Grasp it, and you've lost it. Pluck the rosebud, and it dies."

He looked keenly at his students, to discern how they accepted this concept of nonconsummation, a concept alien to healthy young men in their sexual prime.

Peter Whistler gave a little snort under his breath, his eyes averted. He was the class cynic, contemptuous of everything.

"What was that, Mr. Whistler?" pounced Lewis.

"Nothing, Mr. Lewis," muttered the sullen Whistler.

"If you disagree with me, say so. I can take it," smiled Lewis. He waited for a response, but none was forthcoming. Whistler would not take up the gauntlet; he would rather slouch further down in his chair and sulk.

"Even I can't fight on both sides at once, you know," said Lewis. "That is, I can, but I am liable to win." The students laughed sychophantically, all except Whistler, who regarded Lewis levelly.

Toward noon, C. S. Lewis consulted his gold watch, which hung from a chain and was usually tucked into his jacket's breast pocket. It was now time for his customary stroll to the Eagle and Child for his customary lunch-and-discussion with his customary group of friends before he had to catch the London train for his address this afternoon to the Association of Christian Teachers. At the pub, his friends were already at their regular table, drinking pints of bitter, smoking, arguing and munching on bread and cheese. Christopher Riley, of course, and Rupert Parrish, and Harry Harrington formed, along with Lewis, the core of the group. Today they were joined by Eddie Monk, an Oxford physician, and John Egan, a Scot and a librarian. Clutching his half-pint, Lewis slipped into his seat and lit up his pipe. At once, the usual arguments began.

"The thing is, it's the wardrobe, Jack. I have a complaint about the wardrobe." Monk turned to Lewis, looking for clarification.

"I will not have yet another blasted conversation about Jack's blasted nursery," growled Riley.

"I do have a train to catch, Eddie," said Lewis mildly.

But Monk was deep into his subject and unwilling to let it go. Determined to get his question out into the open, he persisted in the teeth of Riley's scorn. "In the book, you say the house is owned by an old professor, who has no wife. But when the little girl goes into the magic wardrobe, she finds it's full of fur coats."

"Oh, very good, Eddie," Riley applauded sardonically.

"It's simple," said Jack. "They belonged to the professor's old mother."

"Aha!" cried Egan in triumph. "So, to reach the magic world, the child must push through *the mother's fur?*"

The sexual/birth image was not lost on Lewis. "No, no, I won't have that," he scowled, shaking his head. "None of your hand-me-down Freudianism."

Harrington looked startled. "The image is Christian, surely?" he asked.

"No, Harry, it's just itself. It's just . . . magic. Look." Jack Lewis rose from the pub bench and began to act out the scene from *The Lion, the Witch and the Wardrobe*. It was mesmerizing; in less than a minute, the fifty-four-year-old, stocky, gray-haired man had become a child, little Lucy Pevensie struggling to find her way into a magic land.

"The child goes into the wardrobe—the coats are thick, heavy. The fur isn't important, but the idea is weight, something you must push through.

The coats are pressing close, almost suffocating—"
Here Lewis mimed a child being overwhelmed by
the heaviness of the garments and their impenetra-
bility, and his audience watched, rapt.

"And, suddenly, there's white light, crisp, cold
air, trees, snow. Total contrast, you see. The
gateway to a magical world!" His face shone with
the wonder of this magic, and in his emotion he
flung out his arms.

As he did, Jack Lewis saw the time on the wall
clock over the bar. "Lord! My train!" And, jam-
ming on his hat, he bolted.

❦

T W O

Mrs. Gresham

The auditorium was full; almost every seat was occupied. His audience had come to hear Jack Lewis not only because they were familiar with his writings—many were not—and not only because they had listened carefully to his BBC Radio talks on spiritual matters—most had given them one ear only, the other ear cocked for the kettle to boil, or for the husband to demand something, or for the daughter to come downstairs with a blouse to be ironed. No, the audience had come because C. S. Lewis was a genuine literary lion, a celebrity, therefore a genuine coup for their membership.

And they *would* read his books, they vowed to themselves. They would buy them and read them. After all, they were bestsellers. A display table of copies had been set up near the front of the room by the committee. They were for sale, and no doubt Mr. Lewis would be kind enough to autograph them. The titles included: *Mere Christianity, The Problem of Pain, The Screwtape Letters, Miracles, Broadcast Talks, Beyond Personality: the Christian Idea of God.* All the books sounded intimidatingly intellectual, but the audience vowed to themselves that they would persevere.

Meanwhile, there stood C. S. Lewis himself, vigorous and not unhandsome, dressed in his dark lecture suit, his distinguished silver hair brushed neatly back, the very picture of a scholarly Oxford don, his fine hands clasped on the podium, addressing the membership in a deep, dramatic and thrilling voice.

"Yesterday I received a letter that referred to an event that took place nearly a year ago now. December 4th, 1951," he began in a deep voice like dark velvet. "My correspondent hadn't forgotten. I doubt that any of us have. That was the night a Number 1 bus drove into a column of young Royal Marine cadets in Chatham, and killed twenty-four of them. They were ten-year-old boys, marching and singing on their way to a boxing match. The road was unlit. It was a terrible accident. No one to blame . . . except . . ." Here Lewis raised his eyes up to the ceiling of the London lecture hall, obviously passing the buck back up to God.

"The letter asked some simple but fundamental questions. Where was God on that December night? Why didn't He stop it? Isn't God supposed to be good? Isn't He supposed to love us? Does He want us to suffer?" Jack paused for effect, turning the blue searchlights of his eyes full on the audience, which comprised almost all women, middle-class women who sat expectantly, waiting for enlightenment from the celebrated and attractive Mr. C. S. Lewis.

"What if the answer to that question is . . . yes?"

This was the one question that caused the deepest pangs of doubt among Christians, the tenet of faith most difficult to accept. If God is good, why is the world so often evil? Why does God appear indifferent to the suffering of innocents? Why do the wicked go unpunished—even rewarded—while the good are permitted to suffer so much anguish? The three central conclusions in the atheist's arguments against the existence of God are these: if God is all-powerful and can prevent evil, but does *not* prevent evil, then God is not all-loving; if God intends to prevent evil but *cannot*, then God is not all-powerful; if God *does* intend to prevent evil, and is capable of preventing evil, then how can evil exist? That is the hardest question that that nonbelievers ask of Christians. Come to terms with that, and one might come to terms with the infinite.

C. S. Lewis had the answer. In fact, he was something of an expert on this topic, reconciling humankind with an apparently uninvolved deity. "I'm not sure that God particularly wants us to be happy. I think He wants us to be able to love, and be loved. He wants us to . . . grow up." He peered from under his brows at his audience, one of his more effective facial expressions. "Be honest. We're still clinging to childhood, aren't we? We're innocently selfish, we think only of ourselves. We think our toys bring us all the happiness there is, and our nursery is the whole wide world. Something must drive us out of the nursery, to the world of others. And that something is suffering. To put it another way: pain is God's megaphone to rouse a deaf world."

This was one of his most polished and affecting lectures. The concept of God's megaphone was guaranteed to bring comfort to those who asked why? in the face of so much earthly misery. Even these well-dressed and well-fed London women had known sorrow, suffering and loss. Most of them had endured the agony of childbirth, and many of them had lost the fruit of those painful births during the recent war. They had lost husbands, some of them, and nearly all had lost one or more parents. They suffered in the stifling closeness of their marriages to indifferent and unloving men.

Their children, so carefully nurtured, turned out to be selfish and ungrateful. These women, too, were in need of comforting words, and C. S. Lewis was paid to deliver them.

His voice was low, and yet it filled the room, but as he spoke it grew fuller and fuller, like a brazen bell in one of the Oxford chapel towers. "I suggest to you that it's because God loves us that he makes us the gift of suffering. We're like blocks of stone, out of which the sculptor carves the forms of men. The blows of his chisel, which hurt us so much, are what make us perfect."

There was a long silence as he finished, a silence in which the meaning of his words sank in and created an impression never to be erased. The applause, long and loud and sincere, filled the large auditorium, while C. S. Lewis stood there and smiled his thanks.

Jack Lewis picked up the next letter from the slowly diminishing pile of fan mail on his desk and read it.

"A woman has had a dream about me. Writes to ask if I've had a dream about her," he announced to Warnie, who sat across the room reading the *Times*.

Mrs. Young, their long-time housekeeper,

slipped silently into the study to take away the empty coffee cups.

"I had a strange dream last night," Warnie said suddenly.

Now Jack picked the next letter up with a spark of interest, recognizing the blue airmail envelope, the foreign stamps, and the handwriting of the address. "Another dispatch from Mrs. Gresham."

Still musing on his dream, Warnie said, "Can't remember any of it."

"The Jewish Communist Christian American," Jack prompted, thinking it was Mrs. Gresham to whom Warnie was referring, but his brother's mind was still on his dream.

"You may ask me how I know it was a strange dream if I've forgotten it," persisted Warnie. "Can't answer that."

Reading the letter with amusement, Jack Lewis smiled. "I like her letters. She can be quite sharp. Listen to this, Warnie. 'I can't decide whether you'd rather be the child caught in the spell, or the magician casting it.' "

Warnie stuck his nose back in his newspaper, rattling the pages in disapproval. "No news, of course. Never is any."

Jack took off his glasses and swiveled around in his chair to look at Warnie.

"I find that I am quite curious about her."

For the first time, Warnie paid some attention. "About who?"

"Mrs. Gresham." Jack waved the envelope at him. "Her letters are unusual. She writes as if she knows me." He thought about this for a few seconds. "I suppose there is something of me in my books."

"I expect it's just the American style. Americans don't understand about inhibitions." Thus delivered of his opinion, Warnie turned back to his crossword.

Slipping his reading glasses back on, Jack turned to the next page of the letter and uncovered a new fact. "She's called Joy."

"One can't hold her responsible for that," answered Warnie dryly.

"She's coming to England." He glanced up from the letter, surprised. "She's coming to Oxford. She wants to meet us."

Warnie suddenly looked panicked, as though some formidable and aggressive American woman were already outside banging on the front door of The Kilns, ready to storm the defenses of his precious bachelor privacy. "She can't come here," he said in an alarmed voice.

"Oh, no," Jack agreed quickly. "Of course not. She suggests tea in a hotel."

Relieved, Warnie nodded. "Tea is safe. A hotel is safe. Still, she might be quite mad."

Jack took his glasses off again, rubbing the tender spots where they pinched the sides of his nose. He shook his head. "I don't think so. Though she does write poems."

"Poems?!" Warnie's eyebrows rose toward the roots of his thinning hair. "Then she'll be barking!"

"You won't be too agreeable, will you?" Warnie asked anxiously.

"Don't worry, Warnie," said Jack in a soothing voice. It seemed to be his brother's terror that this mad American woman might somehow attach herself to him, and not want to let go. If Jack Lewis was pleasant to her, they'd never be rid of her.

"She'll turn out to be writing a dissertation on wardrobes," predicted Warnie gloomily. "She'll ask if she can come and watch you create. She'll say, 'I'll sit in a corner and you'll never know I'm there.'"

"It's only tea," Jack reassured him. "An hour or so of polite conversation, then we go home, and everything goes on just the way it always has."

The Lewis brothers were waiting for Joy Gresham in the wood-paneled tearoom of Randolph's Hotel, a place where time had stood still since the Edwardian era, where heavy brocaded draperies muffled the tinkle of spoons and the rattle of the cups in the saucers, softened the buzz of conversation and made the music of the solo harpist even more ethereal. At Randolph's, thick Devon cream and fresh strawberry preserves still came with the scones, and the tea sandwiches were still made with cucumbers of fish paste. The recent war and the long period of privation following it seemed to have had little effect on the provincial grandeur and show of this hotel. It seemed that the Randolph had never heard the word "austerity," that grim watchword of the early 1950s in most parts of Britain.

The two men sat at a choice window table facing the room. Behind them across Beaumont Street, through the tall glass panes loomed the majesty of the Ashmolean Museum, its impressive 1841 Greek Revival edifice housing Oxford's rich treasure-trove of art and archeology. Michelangelo drawings, beautiful crafted silver, Flemish masters, and the Alfred Jewel from the ninth century, one of the greatest treasures of Britain's past.

Warnie kept fussing nervously with his silverware, gloomy and anxious, eager to have this tea over with and to get back to The Kilns. A confirmed bachelor and set in his ways, he was uncomfortable with women, especially intelligent women, and he didn't particularly care for Americans. They were loud, brash, overdressed, with braying voices and unintelligible and unbearable accents. Hard on the eyes and even harder on the ears. And this woman, this Mrs. Joy Gresham, sounded especially intimidating, as Jack had described her. Not only an American, but a Jew who had converted to Christianity. And a Communist who wrote poetry, into the bargain. Warnie was fully expecting to be embarrassed by this meal, and believed that nothing good could possibly come of it.

Jack Lewis sat calmly, his eyes on the tearoom entrance. Inside, however, he was feeling a little something of what Warnie was feeling, mingled with his own discomfort. Jack's emotions were mixed—intrigued yet apprehensive. He, too, was having misgivings, was wishing that this occasion were behind him, only a memory. Perhaps he'd been too hasty in agreeing to this meeting. There was a vast difference between exchanging a few friendly words with a fan after one of his talks, and actually sitting down with one over a teapot, face to face, one on one . . . or, rather, one on two, if you counted Warnie. Who knew what this clever woman might be expecting from him?

Jack Lewis was a man who always kept his distance from others, preferring to commune with them intellectually rather than through an expression of feelings. Even his dearest friends knew better than to come too close. Because women were notorious for their emphasis on feelings, Lewis tended to stay away from relationships with them. But he enjoyed a sharp and inquisitive mind, no matter which gender governed it, and he dearly loved a good laugh. This American woman Joy Gresham wrote clever letters that made him laugh, and he found himself a little curious about her, curious enough to agree to have tea with her.

After all, what was the worst thing that could possible come out of this meeting? Say that Mrs. Gresham wanted him to introduce her to his publisher, so that she might have her poetry published here. He could always politely turn her down. Or perhaps the poetry might even be worth recommending. What if she tried to come too close, or attempted to push this simple polite encounter into a continuing sort of friendship? Warnie was right: Americans did tend to get pushy. If Joy Gresham attempted to attach herself to him in some dependent or worshipful way, he would have to be rude, perhaps even brutal in order to send her away. But no doubt it wouldn't come to that. Surely Mrs. Gresham was a civilized woman even if she was an American and would not try to press him into future meetings. Surely C. S. Lewis's treating her to tea today would be enough for her.

He scanned the entranceway, waiting for Mrs. Gresham to appear. She hadn't sent a photograph of herself, so he had no idea what she looked like. A parade of women continually entered the tea-room, in pairs and threes, some alone. Every woman who was by herself stood for a moment in the doorway, scanning the faces in the room, looking for the friend she was supposed to meet. Each time that happened, Jack and Warnie froze, certain that the fat lady in the dreadful hat must be Joy Gresham, or the overdressed woman whose face was thickly plastered with makeup, and who seemed to be making straight for them like a battleship in full array. But it never was.

Warnie picked up his menu. It was almost past his teatime, and he was very hungry. "I wonder if they do toasted tea cakes here," he said seriously, scanning the page.

Jack bent his attention, too, to his menu. Therefore he didn't see the woman who came into the tearoom next. She was not tall, she was slight of build, with large, dark intelligent eyes and thick dark hair showing under a plain velour hat. Her features were lovely, her lips full and her nose high-arched; she resembled a Jewish beauty from the Old Testament, Queen Esther, Judith perhaps, or Rebecca at the well. She was in her late thirties, but still had something left of the bloom of her twenties, although small lines had already begun to creep in around the outer corners of her eyes, and laugh lines reached upward around her mouth.

Joy Davidman Gresham stood uncertainly in the doorway, looking from table to table. She wasn't sure what C. S. Lewis looked like, although she had formed a mental image of him from his writings. There were several middle-aged men in the tearoom, but none of them matched the description in her imagination. She nibbled at her lower lip, wondering what to do. Her heart was pounding with nervousness, and she clutched her handbag tightly to keep her hands still. Perhaps this was all a mistake; perhaps she never should have come.

A waiter was going past, and Mrs. Gresham stopped him. "I'm here to meet Mr. C. S. Lewis, the writer," she said in a low voice.

"Yes, madam."

"Do you know what he looks like?"

"No, madam."

Joy sighed. "He doesn't know what I look like, either."

"Yes, madam," replied the waiter, obviously not at all interested.

"Any ideas?"

"No, madam." And he glided away.

Joy Gresham shrugged her shoulders. She was nothing if not courageous. If nobody was going to find C. S. Lewis for her, she'd have to find him for herself. Raising her voice, she spoke out loudly into the room, "Anybody here called Lewis?"

Like a steel knife slicing through cheese. Mrs. Gresham's loud tones and New York accent sliced through the soft murmurs in the room. Conversation stopped abruptly, teacups were suspended in midair, and every eye turned toward this delicate-boned woman who stood unfazed, head cocked, staring right back at them. Then, slowly, from a table by the window, a man raised his hand like a schoolboy, acknowledging his identity. The Lewis brothers stood up politely as she approached their table.

Lewis had, of course, speculated to himself about how Joy Gresham might look, what sort of features, what color eyes. But, as soon as he saw her, the inevitability of her appearance was stamped upon him. Of course. She couldn't look any possible other way than this.

"You don't look at all like C. S. Lewis," Joy remarked, sitting down. Jack and Warnie took their seats.

"What does C. S. Lewis look like?" asked Jack.

Joy put her head to one side and contemplated the hearty, tailored and clean-shaven man before her. "He's got these really fine features. Wide sensitive eyes. A wild mane of unkempt hair. You know. Poetic. Spiritual." *Shut up, shut up,* she told herself ferociously. *Stop this idiotic line of chatter, you're not being funny, just stupid.* But she was so nervous at finally meeting this man she so admired that she couldn't control her outpouring of talk.

"I'm sorry to disappoint you," Lewis said dryly. "Not to mention the rest of Oxford."

Damn. This was not beginning well, thought Joy. *You had to go and do it, didn't you? Had to open your big New York mouth and embarrass him by yelling out his name where everybody could hear it.* "You don't like it?"

Lewis shrugged almost imperceptibly. "I'm not what you might call a public figure, Mrs. Gresham."

Now Joy Gresham grinned wickedly. "You're not? You write all those books, and give all those talks, just so everyone'll leave you alone?" Her flat New York accent gave her sarcastic words even more thrust.

Touché. Warnie chuckled softly, then buried his head in his menu.

"Dear me," said Jack crisply, nettled. "We've only just met, and already you see through me. Do you drink tea?" He could scarcely conceal his annoyance.

"Of course," Joy answered, just as crisply. "This is England."

"So it is," said Lewis.

We've got to relax a little, though Joy. Or we'll be talking in monosyllables all through tea, and that's not why I came. Out loud, she confessed, "Actually, I'm a little in awe of you, and a little tense, and that always makes me . . . you know . . ." Searching, for the right word, Mrs. Gresham came up instead with a pantomime of a flurry of short jabs and punches. She laughed at herself, and that made Jack and even Warnie laugh with her, breaking the ice. The atmosphere began to thaw, and it seemed that ease might soon be possible.

"It's very childish," Joy admitted. "I'll get over it soon."

"Not too soon, I hope," smiled Lewis. "I like a good fight."

Joy Gresham's large eyes widened. They were the oddest color Lewis had ever seen. From a distance, they appeared to be dark brown, but up close they were actually a very dark gray, with flecks of green, most remarkable. And they were very long eyes, with an outward tilt to the corners, almost Oriental. Now those eyes were fixed on him. "You do?" she asked. "You like a good fight?"

"You sound surprised."

Joy shook her head, but her face still wore a

doubtful expression while mischievous lights danced in her eyes. "No. That's fine. You like a good fight. Great."

Lewis could hear the "but" behind her words. "But . . . ?" he prompted.

She met his eyes. "When did you last lose?" she asked softly.

Touché again. Whatever this woman might be, she was far from stupid. As Lewis had suspected from her letters, she seemed to know him pretty well. He wasn't sure he liked it . . . but, then again, he wasn't sure he didn't.

Now the waiter came up to take their orders. "Yes, Mr. Lewis?"

Joy smiled in triumph. "See? Everyone knows who you are."

Over a traditional full cream tea, with sandwiches, scones, pastries, and several pots of steaming India, the three of them relaxed somewhat, and chatted amiably until the last dollop of Devon had disappeared, and the last cucumber sandwich on brown bread thickly spread with butter had been wolfed down by Warnie. It was time to go.

Oddly enough, Lewis found that he wasn't as eager to be rid of Mrs. Gresham as he'd supposed. The woman possessed great charm and a razor wit, and could speak knowledgeably on a wide range of subjects, returning always to C. S. Lewis's published works, which was flattering. What would be the harm if he showed her the colleges? Who could possibly come to Oxford and not wander over the university's quads and through its wonderful chapels and libraries, gardens and cloisters? At the very least he would show her around Magdalen College, his own precious domain.

Magdalen is pronounced "maudlin," and is not all that ancient as Oxford's colleges go. In 1167 King Henry II issued a decree forbidding English scholars to cross the Channel and study at the Sorbonne. Instead, they set up a seat of learning in the market town of Oxford where the Thames and Cherwell rivers meet, a seat that would eventually comprise some forty colleges. Each college has its own quads and chapels and cloisters and common buildings, and each its own sense of pride.

Merton College lays claim to being the oldest, founded in 1264, its buildings in the soaring Gothic style that characterizes Oxford. Magdalen College was founded almost two centuries later, in 1458, on the banks of the Cherwell. It boasts magnificent gardens, a vast deer park, breathtaking cloisters, and an almost heartbreakingly beautiful Gothic Perpendicular bell tower. Lewis could never walk through its grounds without feeling his heart swell at the splendor of it all, and with the happiness and security of his life here. At Oxford, his own existence seemed to take on the permanence and stability of the buildings' stone walls.

The three of them strolled through the Botanic Garden, emerging through the arch of Danby Gateway to find Magdalen's gargoyle-topped buttresses straight ahead of them.

"It's beautiful," Joy sighed when she saw the college. "How old is it?"

"The college was founded very nearly five hundred years ago," said Lewis with a smile. "Not all of it's that old, of course. My rooms are over there, in the New Building."

Joy Gresham cast an eye on the weathered facade of the so-called New Building. "New, huh?"

"Seventeen thirty-three," said Lewis, and the two of them exchanged a quick grin.

They walked through the college together, Joy looking everywhere and marveling at the beauty she saw. Despite the fact that she was shorter than the two men, her stride matched theirs and she walked well, lightly and quickly, her back held very straight.

"What does your husband do, Mrs. Gresham?" asked Warnie suddenly, to make conversation.

The question appeared to fluster Joy. She stopped, and her brows drew together. "Bill? Bill's . . . a writer."

"And you, too, Jack tells me."

Jack? Joy turned quickly to Lewis. "You call him Jack?"

Lewis shrugged slightly. "I never liked the name Clive," he admitted.

Mrs. Gresham' face lit up like a child's with delight. "Oh, well, if you're a Jack—"

"What?" asked Lewis.

"Well . . . you look *fine* . . . for a Jack." Joy burst into happy laughter as, for the first time since she walked into the Randolph tearoom, she felt perfectly comfortable with the awe-inspiring C. S. Lewis.

As the three of them walked through the Gothic cloisters with their high stone arches and approached the magnificent bell tower, Joy Gresham told the men something about her life in America, and about herself.

"Do you feel like climbing up to the top?" Lewis looked a bit dubious; it was a long, circular climb of many steps, and he sensed that Mrs. Gresham might be too fragile.

"Can one see a view?" she asked.

"Yes, a marvelous view," Jack said with a smile.

"Then, by all means, let's make the journey." She smiled back.

They talked only a little on the way up, saving their breath for the ascent. "Yes, I'm Jewish, but not Jewish-Jewish, if you can follow that," explained Joy as they neared the top. "I was brought up to be a good atheist."

"Atheist?" echoed Jack, surprised.

"Don't sound so shocked."

"I'm not. I was an atheist once." His surprise was that they had this important thing in common, this turning away from disbelief into an acceptance of Christian doctrine.

Now it was Mrs. Gresham's turn to be surprised. "You don't say? So we're both lapsed atheists."

Lewis drew a trifle back from her eagerness. "But I was never a Communist."

"Why not?" demanded Joy.

"What do you mean, 'Why not?' "

"Back in '38, surely the choice was be a fascist and conquer the world, or be a Communist and save it?" Joy Gresham was utterly serious; she seemed to perceive the black and the white, but hardly any of the myriad shades of gray in between.

"Is that so?" said Jack Lewis dryly. "I must have been otherwise occupied at the time."

Slightly out of breath, the trio emerged out onto the top level of the bell tower, a broad parapet. Joy appeared tired, and she looked around for somewhere to perch, settling finally on the low stone wall around the parapet. Gazing out over the university and the city of Oxford, she could see the ancient buildings of the colleges and the green of the gardens and swards. Around her, spires of stone stretched their lacily carved towers up to heaven, cherubs and gargoyles alike aspiring to reach God. Everywhere she looked Joy found breathtaking beauty and the overwhelming sense of centuries gone by.

"Now, there's a world worth saving," she murmured, half to herself.

Pleased by her enthusiastic reaction to his beloved Oxford, Jack felt himself warming to her. "At dawn, on the first of May every year, the choristers from the choir school stand up here and sing to the rising sun. I'm told they draw quite a crowd."

"What do they sing?" asked Joy eagerly.

"I can't say I've ever risen early enough to hear them," Jack confessed.

"Why not? It sounds wonderful." She could picture the choristers in their robes—blue and gold, like the heavens?—while their high pure voices chanted in Latin a hymn of praise to the rising sun. She could feel in her bones the damp chill of six o'clock of an English morning, the stars still out, the sky still almost black, but in the east the first pink threads of Aurora's dawn-robe making their shy appearance. Joy could also imagine the sober dons in their black gowns and scarlet hoods, listening rapt, understanding the Latin words of the song. But C. S. Lewis was not among them.

Lewis shrugged. "I don't really go in for seeing the sights."

A flicker of annoyance at his snobbery rose in Joy Gresham like a tiny flame. "So what *do* you do?" she challenged him. "Walk around with your eyes shut?"

Taken aback, Jack Lewis could only blink at her. "You know, Mrs. Gresham, I almost don't know what to say to you."

"Good Lord!" Warnie whispered to himself. He had never heard his brother confess anything like that before. And to a woman! My word!

They stood on the railway station platform, waiting for Mrs. Gresham's train to London.

"How long do you plan to stay in England?" asked Jack.

"Till the end of December," Joy replied quietly.

"Do you expect to be in Oxford again?"

"I don't know." Joy's long eyes tilted up at him expectantly. "I could be," she said carefully.

"What do you say, Warnie?" Jack said heartily. "Do you think we could rise to a pot of home-brewed tea?"

"I think we can manage that," replied Warnie,

only mildly surprised. He was half expecting something of this kind, half dreading it. This woman was a little too clever, a little too attractive, and a little too outspoken for his taste. Not to mention that dreadful American accent. Still, she was damned lively and interesting.

"Given adequate warning, of course," Jack added.

Mrs. Gresham smiled, pleased at the invitation, which she hadn't dared to expect, although she was very much hoping for it. "Could I bring my son? Douglas is the biggest fan of your Narnia books. I know he'd really like to meet you."

C. S Lewis bowed his head politely. "Of course."

Issuing great puffs of steam, the fast train to London came puffing into the station. Joy Gresham held out her hand. "Thank you, Mr. Lewis. I've enjoyed meeting you."

Jack took her hand in his and shook it. Joy's hand was small, thin, with prominent bones, but her handshake wasn't delicate, it had firmness and even strength. "We shall see you soon, then. Safe journey."

Joy turned to Warnie. "Goodbye, Major Lewis."

Warnie inclined his head gravely. "Mrs. Gresham."

Climbing into the train, Joy Gresham went in search of a seat. For a minute, Jack and Warnie stood on the platform, watching her. Jack looked uncomfortable. "What does one do?" he asked his brother. "Wait for the train to leave?"

It was not a familiar situation, seeing off a woman. Had the passenger been a male friend or colleague, they would have seen him aboard and headed for home at once. But was it incumbent on a gentleman to stand and wait until the lady had actually left the station?

Warnie shrugged, and turned to go. With a feeling of relief, Jack followed. Yet, relief wasn't the only emotion he was feeling. Joy Gresham had succeeded in annoying him, and intriguing him. He was actually rather looking forward to seeing her again.

THREE

Tea at the Kilns

With Joy Gresham back in London, events returned to their preferred snail's pace at The Kilns. Autumn with its chilly mists and falling leaves closed in around the house. The curtains were daily drawn earlier and earlier, and the coal fires were lit on the hearths a few minutes sooner every evening. The first hard frost killed the dahlias, turning their ebullient petals black and withered overnight, and Paxton, their aged gardener, dug them up and put them in the shed to store for the winter.

But the old roses, as if in defiance of the weather, put forth a remarkable show of autumnal bloom, and the spreading masses of sedum shone a bright coppery red. And the chrysanthemums, the "gold flowers" of the ancient Greeks, burst into blossom with wonderful colors of bronze and gold, maroon and imperial purple. Quarreling birds foraged in the trees for late ash berries and wild cherries and soon they'd be fighting over the holly berries.

As the days grew shorter, Warnie Lewis spent more time occupying his desk across from Jack's; sometimes he worked on the manuscript of his laborious French history, more often he just sat quietly in his big chair, smoking his pipe, sipping his whiskey, and reading contentedly by lamplight until it was time to fill the hot water bottles for bed. Warnie never said much in any case, and he said nothing at all about Mrs. Gresham. He appeared to have forgotten all about her.

Jack, however, resented the shortening of the days. Every waking moment was a precious commodity. He was kept entirely busy, with his radio talks and lectures, his classes, his tutorials, and his life at Oxford. In addition, he was wrapped up in writing his new book, the fourth volume in the series *The Chronicles of Narnia.* This one was to be called *The Silver Chair,* and it occupied almost all of the hours he spent away from the college.

Surrounded by illustrations and maps of his own enchanted land, he wrote and wrote, and he, too, never mentioned Joy Gresham. Although he hadn't forgotten her. From time to time the thought of her did flash across his mind and flicker out again. But with no real significance, or so he believed.

Simply idle curiosity. An interesting person, and one with strong and definite beliefs. He'd enjoyed talking to her.

It seemed to Lewis that Joy Gresham possessed an earthiness, a direct bluntness, that was refreshing after the brittle and oblique academic wit of his friends and colleagues at Oxford. Joy struck him as somebody who would say what she thought, without hesitation, and without the icy politesse of the upperclass Briton who was so familiar to Jack. She was unlike anybody else he'd ever met, but whether he could attribute her differences to her being American, Jewish, or simply herself, he couldn't say.

The Oxford seminars on poetry continued, with the same group of students—Frith, Standish, Lieven, and, of course, the rebel pupil Whistler, who today appeared to be sound asleep in his chair.

"Character and plot. Chicken and egg. Which comes first?" asked Professor Lewis, brandishing his copy of Aristotle's *Poetics*. He stopped, as though expecting an intelligent answer, but his students, well trained by now, waited obediently to hear it from the horse's mouth.

"Aristotle's solution was simple and radical. He said: plot *is* character. Forget psychology. Forget the inside of men's heads. Read them by their actions." Lewis turned to look hard at Whistler, and his class did the same.

"For example, Mr. Whistler is asleep," he continued. "From that action, I know that he has no interest in what I have to say. The puzzle is, that being the case, why is he here at all? So we construct a plot from Mr. Whistler's actions. He comes. He sleeps. Aristotle would say that the next question is not 'Why?' but 'What will Mr. Whistler do next?' "

Then, as though the eyes staring at him had a physical impact on him, Peter Whistler opened his own eyes. Seeing everybody staring, his cheeks turned a dull red.

"My classes are not compulsory, Mr. Whistler," said C. S. Lewis in an affable voice, but really genuinely offended. "Nor are my chairs very comfortable. I suggest—"

Pulling himself up out of his chair, the rebellious Whistler gathered up his notebooks, his texts, and his jacket. The embarrassed expression on his face was now replaced by its usual look of sullenness. "All right. I'm going." He left the room, closing the door behind him with a bang. Lewis turned back to his class and shrugged broadly.

"He comes. He sleeps. He goes. The plot thickens."

* * *

After an exchange of friendly letters, Jack Lewis finally issued an official invitation for Joy Gresham and her son Douglas to come to tea at The Kilns, and it had been accepted with pleasure. A date had been set and now the day had finally arrived. It was a chilly day in early November, but mercifully a dry one. The drawing room, though, *was* on the damp side, because it was a room largely unused. Which was strange, because it was a room almost exactly like the study, with tall bookshelves stacked high with old volumes, and magazines and papers scattered everywhere. The only difference was that the furniture in this room was less shabby and rather more comfortable than the chairs in the study. And there was a large wireless on a side table, over which Warnie would sometimes listen to Jack when he was broadcasting over the BBC. But the habits of old bachelors die hard, and the study was the preferred room in which the Lewis brothers spent most of their time.

With guests already on their way, Jack Lewis set himself the task of warming the parlor with a generous fire. He laid the kindling with care, and had just finished building a large pile of pieces of soft coal in a pyramid on top of the kindling when Mrs. Young came in with the heavy tray of tea things, followed by Warnie carrying a cut-glass cake stand on which sat a plump Dundee cake, baked by their housekeeper especially for the occasion.

The look on Warnie's face was gloomy and apprehensive, and although he said nothing as he set the cake down on the tea table, Jack knew his brother well, and after so many years together could almost read his thoughts. Warnie was not only uncomfortable with Mrs. Gresham coming here today, he was uncomfortable with the very *idea* of Mrs. Gresham.

"It's all right, Warnie. She sails back to New York after Christmas. One can be so much more friendly to people who can't stay long."

Jack intended his brother to be reassured, but Warnie was not convinced. "I wonder what her husband thinks of her gallivanting around England like this."

"This isn't the Middle Ages, Warnie," said Jack in mild reproof. Warnie, with his small experience of the outside world and its modern changes, was given to some dust-covered Victorian opinions. He recognized that Joy Gresham was both intelligent and vivacious, but Warnie had never found either quality particularly appealing in a woman; on the contrary, they were characteristics he found intimidating. That Jack should be attracted to them was a complete and rather unpleasant mystery to him.

"I bet you ten bob she'll make you listen to one of her poems. Then she'll say to you, 'How did you like it, Mr. Lewis?' and you'll be stumped." It was a dire prophecy, but Jack met it with calmness.

"I shall say, 'Only you could have written that.' " At that moment, as if in contradiction to Lewis's coolness, the carefully laid fire collapsed, spilling large, dusty black pieces of coal onto the hearth rug.

"Blast!" Jack knelt to retrieve the coal just as the taxi from the station was heard pulling up to the front gate. The guests were here. Warnie left the room to go and greet them, while Jack made a hurried effort to put the damned fire back to rights.

Mrs. Gresham was just paying off the taxi when Warnie emerged from the house, and her son, wearing some odd American plaid jacket and buffalo-check cap with earflaps, came running up the path.

"Hello, you must be Douglas." Warnie rather liked children, in a distant way. Other people's children. When they were well behaved. When they were taken away again in a very short while by their mothers.

The little boy, an auburn-haired chap of about ten, was looking up at Warnie with awestruck expectancy. "Are you him?" he breathed.

64

"No, I'm his brother," smiled Warnie. "So you found us, Mrs. Gresham," he said to Joy.

"It isn't hard when you know where to look," Joy smiled back.

Although she appeared calm, inside Joy Gresham was terribly nervous. Her admiration and respect for C. S. Lewis was boundless, and to be actually invited into his home, his private sanctum, was intimidating. Joy knew that she was totally unlike the English ladies who presumably came to tea, with their clipped accents and their bottomless fund of trivial chatter. Joy had no patience for small talk; inside her breast intensity burned like a white-hot flame. It was an intensity that often frightened people away, and she didn't want that to happen between her and Lewis. In addition to respecting him, she liked him very much, and she had too few friends here in England. Could they possibly become friends, the Jewish Communist Christian American and the celebrated author and Oxford don? *Don't mess things up*, she warned herself.

The three of them entered the house. Warnie led the way to the drawing room, where Jack was still on his knees on the hearth rug, his hands covered in coal dust.

"That's him," said Warnie in a whisper to Douglas, as though pointing out some mythical creature.

Embarrassed, Jack Lewis struggled to his feet, took his pocket handkerchief out, and began rubbing the dirt off his hands. His face was red and his hair was out of place, an entirely different look from his customary immaculate appearance.

"Here you are, then. Good, good." Shyly, Jack put his hand out to shake Joy's, but seeing how filthy it was, he drew it back and surreptitiously wiped it on his trousers.

"We really appreciate this, Mr. Lewis," said Joy Gresham. "You've no idea how much Douglas has been looking forward to today."

"So this is Douglas." The boy was gazing at him so intensely it seemed to Jack he was trying to memorize his features.

Douglas turned and whispered to his mother. "Will he write in my book?"

"Ask him." Joy gave her son a little push forward. But the boy was too bashful to say anything to so admired a writer. He just held his book up silently.

"I told him you'd write in his Narnia book. I hope you don't mind."

Smiling, Lewis took the offered book. It was *The Lion, the Witch and the Wardrobe.* "Douglas, yes?" He reached in his jacket for a pen, rummaging through pocket after pocket until he found one.

Again, Douglas whispered to his mother. "And

he wants to know, do you have an attic?" Joy interpreted.

"We do." Jack finished writing and handed the book to the boy just as the housekeeper came in with the steaming teapot. "There you are. Thank you, Mrs. Young."

"What did he write?" Joy asked her son.

The boy read out the inscription. " 'The magic never ends.' "

"If it does, sue him," said Joy.

"I'd sure like to see the attic." This time, Douglas Gresham spoke up for himself.

"Then you shall," smiled Warnie. Taking the boy by the shoulder, he led him out of the room, turning at the door to speak a word to Joy. "Jack is particularly hoping you'll introduce him to your poetry." It was a parting shot meant to get back at his brother—if only a little—for introducing strangers into his home.

"Don't worry," Joy said, eyeing Jack shrewdly. "I don't inflict my poems on innocent strangers."

"Not strangers, I hope," Lewis said with politeness. "And I would be interested to know about your poems. What about some of the long-promised tea?" He poured a cup for her. "Do you take milk?"

"Yes, please. So, what do you want to 'know about' my poems? How long they are? Their rhyme schemes? Their major influences?"

Her sarcasm was an effective reproach for his patronizing tone. He deserved it, and he knew it. Jack Lewis had the grace to blush, if not actually then metaphorically. "I'm sorry. You're quite right. Would you be so kind as to introduce me to the poems themselves?"

"I'm not sure." It wasn't a coy statement, but a matter-of-fact one. Joy Davidman Gresham was never coy, as Jack Lewis was coming to learn.

"I won't be rude about them."

"So what will you do? Stay silent, or tell lies?" Her American bluntness made his English politeness seem somehow effete.

Lewis thought for a second. "I shall choose after I've heard one."

Joy couldn't help but grin. It was exactly the answer she would have given in his place. "Okay. Why not? I *have* actually won a national poetry award. Shared with Robert Frost." She said it with quiet pride, and with mischievous lights in her eyes.

"I'm impressed." Jack even looked impressed.

Joy's grin widened. "Let's hope you stay that way. I'll give you an early one, so I'm covered. I wrote this when I was twenty-two, Spanish Civil War. It's called *Snow in Madrid*." Taking a deep breath, she recited softly and without dramatic emphasis.

" 'Softly, so casual,
Lovely, so light, so light,
The cruel sky lets fall
Something one does not fight.

Men before perishing
See with unwounded eye
For once, a gentle thing
Fall from the sky.' "

Joy finished reciting, and waited for a reaction. Lewis said nothing. "Embarrassed, huh? Well, buddy, you asked for it, you get out of it."

"No," he answered quietly. "I'm touched."

"Touched?" Joy Gresham lifted one eyebrow. Then she nodded, accepting his reaction. "Okay, that'll do. That's about its level. When was I ever in Madrid?" she asked rhetorically, as if to fend off the same question from Lewis.

"Personal experience isn't everything," spoke the Oxford don who dwelled almost exclusively in the world of books.

"I disagree," Joy replied swiftly and with emphasis. "I think personal experience is everything."

"So reading is a waste of time?" It was a challenge, from one literate person to another.

"Not a waste of time," Joy admitted thoughtfully. "But reading's safe, isn't it? Books aren't about to hurt you."

"Why should one want to be hurt?" Jack asked softly.

"That's when you learn."

"Just because something hurts, it doesn't make it more true. Or more significant." Their conversation was taking on the aspect of dialogue, of stichomythia, with ideas snapping back and forth between them in clipped lines.

Joy was surprised by the sharpness in his voice. "No, I guess not," she conceded.

Jack Lewis continued, pressing the subject. "I'm not saying pain is purposeless, or even neutral. But to find meaning in pain, there has to be something else. Pain is a tool. If you like, pain is God's mega—"

" 'God's megaphone to rouse a deaf world,' " quoted Joy.

"How embarrassing." Jack bit his lip and turned his eyes away from her. "You know my writing too well."

But Joy wasn't feeling triumph just because she'd caught C. S. Lewis out in self-citation. If *he* didn't have the right to quote himself, then who did? "I guess I've read most of it. I knew you pretty well before we met."

Lewis smiled. "Ah, but you had not had the 'personal experience.' " His tone put the words into quotation marks, a gentle mockery.

"Mr. Lewis—listen, I can't go on calling you Mr. Lewis. It makes me feel like a kid. Can I call you Jack?"

Lewis hesitated only a fraction of a second. "Of course," he said quietly, but his mind was disquieted. First the poem, now the familiarity. This woman was breaking down one by one the barriers he'd so carefully erected around himself. He would have to be more careful around her, even though she was proving to be even more interesting than he had first supposed.

"Jack, I'm Joy." She held her hand out for him to shake and Jack, embarrassed at the thought of touching her, took her hand and gave it a brief shake.

"So, Jack," she said with that tilt of the head that he was coming to recognize as a signal that she was about to dare him, "have you ever been really hurt?"

"You don't give up, do you?" said Lewis with an admiring smile.

"Does anybody ever come up here?" Douglas Gresham asked breathlessly.

"Not anymore," replied Warnie, almost as if he regretted the fact. But it was a long climb up from the ground floor, and neither of the brothers was young anymore, or had any more need of the abandoned possessions stored up here.

The boy entered the attic of The Kilns with an air of reverent expectancy. He couldn't believe that he was really in the home of C. S. Lewis himself, the magician, the enchanter whose books had carried Douglas out of the mundane and often unhappy world in which he was forced to live, and brought him into the otherworld of Narnia, where lions talked and children could be free to do wonderful things. And this was the real attic, filled with mysterious old trunks, with long-outgrown and discarded toys and books, raggedy once-beloved stuffed animals, bits and pieces of broken furniture, framed photographs with faded faces peering out. A magical attic.

And there—Douglas could hardly credit the evidence of his eyes—there in the far corner of the wonderfully cluttered space was a wardrobe. A tall wooden wardrobe, just like the one in the book. Could this be *the* wardrobe?

Douglas Gresham looked at Warnie, his eyes round, and the question was unspoken. But C. S. Lewis's brother knew exactly what the boy was asking silently. Was this the very wardrobe from *The Lion, the Witch and the Wardrobe*? He smiled quietly, as if to say "Who knows?" Let the lad believe in magic as long as he was able to.

* * *

Joy Gresham and Jack Lewis wandered from the drawing room across the drafty hallway and into the study, so that Lewis could show her where he did his writing. Joy looked around her avidly, drinking in the atmosphere. There were books everywhere, stacks of papers, the pervading smell of stale smoke, two desks, two chairs, *as though the Lewis brothers were two bears out of a fairy tale*, thought Joy with a secret smile. It was altogether a room with an air of being lived in and worked in. A satisfying study for a writer.

Close to Jack's desk hung a framed picture, a watercolor of great peace, suffused with sunlit quietude. Joy went nearer to inspect it. " 'The Golden Valley,' " she read from the little brass nameplate tacked to the picture frame. "Where's that?"

"Somewhere in Herefordshire, I believe."

"Somewhere special?" She turned to look at Jack.

"In a way. It was on our nursery wall when I was a child. I didn't know it was a real place then. I thought it was a view of heaven."

Joy studied the picture carefully, as if trying to see it through the boy Jack Lewis's childish eyes. "The Promised Land," she whispered, mostly to herself.

He nodded gravely. "I used to think that one day I'd come round a bend in the road, or over the brow of a hill, and there it would be," Jack said in a tone that could only be described as nostalgic. Then, with hesitation, he added softly, "I . . . have been . . . really hurt, you know. The first time is always the worst. That was when my mother died."

Joy had the instinctive feeling that Jack rarely spoke about this, if ever. She felt a thrill of gratitude that he had shared this with her, a virtual stranger. A connection was being made here, an important personal event in her life was taking place right this minute. Was it happening for him, too? "How old were you?"

"Nine."

"Old enough to hurt," she said gently, yet with a bitterness under the words the meaning of which he didn't fathom now, although later he was to learn its significance.

"Oh, yes. It was the end of my world," Jack said from very far away. "I remember my father in tears. Voices all over the house. Doors shutting and opening. It was a big house, all long empty corridors. I remember I had the toothache. I wanted my mother to come to me. I cried for her to come, but she didn't come." He fell silent, turning his face away from Joy Gresham's sympathetic gaze.

Jack Lewis had no idea why he had opened himself up to her like this; after all, they were virtual strangers to each other. Perhaps it was to dispel her mistaken belief that his life had been untouched by sorrow, pain, or loss. But why should he care what she thought? He couldn't say. All he knew was that he had the almost-unprecedented impulse to share his emotions with Joy Gresham. Lewis never talked about his feelings; indeed, he tended to disapprove of feelings, much preferring rational thought.

"And after death?" Joy asked softly. "Did you believe you'd meet her again?" She was imagining, quite vividly, the deep sorrow and loneliness the little boy Jack must have suffered, and her maternal heart went out to him in sympathy. She could actually picture him sitting there, his swollen jaw aching, his heart torn into pieces, small and miserable and desperately afraid.

Jack Lewis shook his head. "No, I don't think I had any faith in anything when I was a child. She was gone. That was all." He roused himself as if from a revery. "You should have a look round the garden before you go."

But Joy wasn't ready to let go yet. As Jack had said, she didn't give up. "And you still listen for the footsteps coming down the corridor. And they still don't come."

75

Joy Gresham's words stopped Jack Lewis dead in his tracks. He felt sudden tears stinging his eyes behind his lids, and he struggled to keep them down. What she said was true, absolutely true. He was astonished by the swiftness and depth of this woman's understanding. He knew she must be gazing at him with those remarkable dark grey eyes, but he still couldn't look at her. "Yes," he answered at last, in a stifled voice.

"So show me the garden."

While Jack and Joy had been talking in the study, Douglas had gone out to explore, with Warnie as his guide. Now the youngster came running down the garden path towards them, his face shining with boyish excitement.

"There's a lake, mom. A wood with a lake."

"It's really a flooded clay-pit," Lewis explained. "For the old brickworks."

"You be careful, Douglas!" called Joy as her son pelted back toward the water. Having been relieved of child care, Warnie headed back to the house and the comfort gained from a large whisky on a chilly day.

"Does he miss home?" asked Jack, who was beginning to feel a sort of kinship with the boy.

Joy Gresham's lovely face clouded. "Oh, sure. He'd like to be home for Christmas, but . . . well . . . it hasn't turned out that way." Her words were flat and toneless, but Jack could sense a deep well of unhappy emotion underneath them, and her sadness moved him.

"So what are you doing for Christmas?" he asked.

"Some lucky English hotel, I expect. That should be a new experience." She shrugged wryly.

"And your husband will have to shift for himself."

Joy cast a sharp glance at Jack, checking to see if his words carried a hidden meaning. But the remark was perfectly innocent; it meant nothing more than it said. "Yes. He's pretty good at that." Once again that flatness of tone, masking an unknown meaning.

By now they had reached the lake and walked out onto the jetty, where Douglas crouched, gazing with fascination into the dark, still water.

"The lake is much older than the house, of course," Jack Lewis explained. "They say Shelley used to sail paper boats here."

"Made of early drafts of his poems, no doubt," laughed Joy. Jack laughed with her.

Lewis hesitated a moment, then, with sudden inspiration, plunged ahead. "You know, I don't like to think of you Christmasing in an hotel. Why don't you come here? You'd be very welcome." His words were sincere, although the feelings behind them were somewhat ambivalent. Jack *did* want to see Joy Gresham again; he just didn't quite understand why. It was much easier for him to chalk his feelings up to friendliness and sympathy. She was, after all, a woman on her own in a foreign country. And his only intent was to be a gentleman and a fellow writer.

"No, no." Joy shook her head vehemently. "You don't want a couple of Yankees rampaging all over your house." Even though out of politeness she felt obligated to decline, her heart gave a leap in her breast, and the flatness left her voice. Jack Lewis's invitation flattered and delighted her, and what Joy really wanted to say was "Yes, yes! Of course I'll come!"

"I'll have to ask Warnie, of course," Jack continued, as though she hadn't spoken. "But speaking for myself, I would welcome the company. Somehow Christmas makes more sense when there are children around."

Joy's spirit flooded with happiness. She hadn't made a mess of today after all. She was so afraid that she'd offended Jack Lewis, whom she admired so greatly, with her challenges and her blunt observations. She knew she had a big mouth; she understood how intimidating she could be, especially to men who were unused to women, or who had preconceived notions about a woman's place in the universe. But she couldn't help herself; what she thought, she said.

Also, Joy Gresham recognized the walls which Jack Lewis had built around himself. She had seen blocks of stone like those before, built up around the human spirit to keep others at a distance. Joy had read before this the frightened warning sign that says "Keep Out." And yet, here he was, willing to see her again, even inviting her back to his home.

"I suppose we ought to get a tree," muttered Warnie.

"What I resent," Christopher Riley pronounced decisively, "is the general presumption of goodwill. I feel no goodwill towards my fellow men whatever. I feel ill will." His sardonic brows were drawn together in his trademark scowl.

"It's nothing to do with how you feel, Christopher," retorted Jack Lewis. "Feelings are far too unreliable." This was a central tenet of Lewis's belief system; weigh rational thought against human emotion, and the balance would tip in favor of thought every time.

"Most of the Christmas spirit ends up in my surgery, anyhow," said Dr. Monk glumly.

"It will be different this year, I've no doubt.

More cheerful," Warnie said without much conviction or cheer.

"What's that, Warnie?" asked Monk.

"The festive season."

They were seated at their customary table in the Eagle and Child pub close by Magdalen College, smoking, drinking bitter out of pewter mugs, and eating cheese on hard rolls. Today the group was smaller than usual, numbering only Jack and Warnie, Christopher, and the chaplain Harry Harrington from the college, and Eddie Monk. It was only a few days before Christmas and the pub was brightly decorated for the holidays with pine boughs and holly berries, and rather tatty garlands of tinsel saved from prewar days. Perhaps because of the close approach of the holidays, the Eagle and Child was jammed solid with drinkers, all of them talking at high volume. The little group at the table had had to wait an unconscionable ten minutes for the next round of drinks.

"I'm afraid Christmas as I remember it is something of a lost cause," put in Harry Harrington.

"That's because we've lost the magic," said Jack.

"Oh, no more blasted magic, please!" Christopher Riley moaned, casting his eyes up to a deaf heaven. Christmas spirit or no Christmas spirit, he was fed up with his friend's forays into nowhere-land.

But Jack Lewis would not be put off. "No, it's true. Tell people it's about being kind to the poor and needy, and naturally they don't even listen," said Jack. "Do they?"

"The poor and needy *do* come into it," the chaplain protested. "No room at the inn, remember? For mother and child."

"Jack's invited them to stay with us," Warnie said, swallowing a mouthful of beer.

"Who?" asked Harrington.

"Mother and child," answered Warnie with a touch of irony that was unusual in his blunt self.

"Mrs. Gresham and her son. They're spending Christmas with us," Jack filled in reluctantly. He knew that this would bring on a rash of questions, especially from his close friend the skeptic Christopher Riley, and so it did.

Riley's eyelid usually kept deliberately half closed, snapped open in astonishment. Jack Lewis, the duke of detachment, the high priest of privacy, had invited a houseguest! And a female houseguest to boot! And with a child! At this rate, wonders never would cease! "Well, Jack, you have succeeded in surprising me. Who is Mrs. Gresham?"

Even Harry Harrington, always Jack Lewis's champion, especially in matters of faith, appeared astonished by the news. A wave of embarrassment washed over Lewis without his really knowing why.

How to explain her so that his friends wouldn't come away with the wrong idea?

"Just a friend. An American, A writer," he mumbled. He looked around the table at his companions, to find them all staring solemnly at him. They'd got hold of the wrong end of the stick after all.

Jack Lewis found himself on the defensive, and his chin went up in defiance. "People *do* have guests at Christmas," he added, challenging his friends to contradict him.

"Not under any circumstances, ever!" Riley declared. "Not even in Tuscany!"

"Well, we're having guests," insisted Jack. "It's not at all unusual."

Warnie uttered a small snort of disbelief and took another mouthful of bread and cheese. He thought Jack protested far too much.

F O U R

Christmas

It began to snow during the second week of December. Not hard, but steadily, and for several days. When it finally stopped, the weather stayed very cold so the snow, deeply drifted in places, remained on the ground. Outside Oxford, on Headington Hill and around The Kilns, the icy cover was still a crystalline white, but in the city itself it soon turned into a grimy slippery slush, making for rough going. The Oxford students' bicycles stayed locked in their racks outside the college buildings, as the young men and women, wrapped up in their six-foot-long striped mufflers, went slogging from classroom to library to don's study on foot. The local cafés did a brisk business in hot cocoa and mugs of steaming sweet tea, while the chemists stocked up on aspirin and vitamin C powders.

Then, just as everybody was getting ready to

celebrate a white Christmas of the variety prettily depicted on holiday cards, the sun began to shine. Day after day the sky was a bright, crisp blue, and the sun poured its shorter winter rays down steadily. Until all the snow was melted away, even on the icy heights outside Oxford. What was left in its place was mud. It was going to be a muddy Christmas.

Jack Lewis kicked the slippery mud off his heavy shoes as he entered the cavernous cold of the station. Even inside the building, he could still see his breath condensing in the air. Jack hadn't intended to meet Joy's train, but as the hour approached for her arrival, he found himself heading for the railway station, and then actually being there, pretending to thumb through magazines at the newsagent's stall.

Lewis couldn't account for his embarrassment at being here, so he decided that his embarrassment didn't exist. He honestly didn't comprehend that, had Joy Gresham been some visiting male professor, or a male writer or editor, or an unattractive female, he wouldn't be at all self-conscious about meeting this train. He would have arrived on the platform early, scanning the carriages eagerly for his arriving guest. Now, in fact, he was rather pretending to be somewhere else, as though the London train had nothing at all to do with him. As usual, Jack's emotions were a mystery he kept hidden from himself.

The station was crowded with last-minute travelers going somewhere to spend Christmas. Noisy groups of students invaded the platforms to take the trains or merely to say goodbye to the departees or hello to the arrivees. Holiday-makers carried brightly wrapped packages and moved with an air of expectation. As for his own expectation, Jack didn't have long to wait. With a loud whistle and a long exhalation of steam, Joy Gresham's train pulled in. An outpouring of passengers began to stream onto the platform, claiming their parcels and luggage and heading for the exits. Without actually approaching the train, Jack had stationed himself where the passengers would have to walk past him to get to the exit gates.

Joy Gresham and her son descended from a second-class carriage, each of them carrying a small suitcase. For a few seconds, Jack stood watching them from a distance, noticing again Joy's graceful movements and her quick smile as she shared a private joke with Douglas. She had evidently made friends with other passengers on the journey, because she was bidding an elderly couple goodbye and happy holidays. Her face was so alive, her expression so appealing! He relished this quiet moment alone before they would finally come face-to-face. Although he didn't realize it, Jack enjoyed looking at Joy Gresham.

"Jack! You shouldn't have!" Joy's face lit up with surprise and delight as she saw Jack Lewis coming toward her on the platform.

"Hallo, Joy, Douglas. Let me take that." He held his hand out, but before Joy could clasp it, he took their two suitcases and turned to lead the way. Since the Lewises didn't own a car, they journeyed to The Kilns by taxicab. After greeting Warnie and Mrs. Young, Joy and Douglas followed Jack up the narrow staircase to the floor where the bedrooms were. Jack put the suitcases down on the landing and opened one door, and then a second.

"Joy here." Jack turned away quickly, averting his eyes from Joy's room, oddly embarrassed by the reality that a woman would be sleeping in that room. "Douglas here." He opened a third door, across the hall. "Bathroom here. And, well, that's that."

"Fine." Joy picked up her case and carried it into the room that had been named as hers. It was a spacious room, decently furnished, with a large window looking out on what, in spring, would be a lovely garden. Right now, the view was of a sea of mud.

"Good, good." Jack rubbed his hands together nervously. "We'll leave you to settle in, then."

Downstairs, he consulted his brother anxiously. "What do you think next, Warnie? A cup of tea?"

Warnie thought the question over and nodded. "Can't go too far wrong with a cup of tea."

As before, they had their tea in the drawing room, with Mrs. Young serving. The housekeeper could barely keep her eyes off Joy Gresham. As she put down the tray of sandwiches, she stared. What were things coming to? In all her years at The Kilns, she had never once seen a female house-guest. And a Yank in the bargain! On her way back to the kitchen, Mrs. Young kept glancing at Joy nervously as though the American woman were suddenly going to sprout a pair of horns.

Joy huddled in a large chair as close to the fire as she could come, trying to get warm in this unheated house. Unable to get used to the dampness of the English climate, she hadn't been warm since she came to Britain. Keeping her hands wrapped around her teacup as though the very touch of the hot liquid could bring relief to the chill in her bones, she took deep, grateful sips of the tea. Douglas, who had almost acclimatized to British damp, sat in the window seat, looking out at the mud and wishing for snow.

Jack handed Joy the dish of scones. "We're invited to a social occasion this evening. Don't suppose you'd care to come?"

"With Douglas?"

"Ah," was all he uttered, but his little added shrug said plainly, "Sorry, no."

Joy shook her dark head. "You go without me, Jack. I could do with an early night."

"No, no," Jack said hastily. "It's nothing of any importance. Just a drink at the college."

"We could always ask Mrs. Young," suggested Warnie, who'd been looking forward to the evening. Although he was familiar to all of Jack's fellow dons, Warnie could never turn up at a college do without his brother, and it was evident that Jack would not go without Joy. It would be inexcusably rude to his guest. "We'd be back by nine."

"I'll be okay, you go, Mom." This from Douglas.

"No, no, I was being thoughtless," Jack said weakly. "You've only just arrived." And so, with this mild formal protest, it was settled. The three adults would go to the party, and Douglas would remain behind with the housekeeper.

The boy was already tucked up in bed with a book when Joy, her hair arranged differently and her coat buttoned over her party dress, came in to kiss him good night. "You're sure aobut this, now? I don't have to go." She searched her son's face anxiously.

"Mom, you're going."

"Got your hot water bottle?"

Reaching under the covers, he pulled out an ancient rubber hot water bottle wrapped in a flannel. "Why do you think they don't heat the house?"

Joy shook her head, trying not to laugh. "This is a very strange country, darling. But I think the natives are friendly."

When they arrived at the college, the porter greeted the Lewis brothers with his usual courtesy. But when he caught sight of the slender woman in the dark coat, his jaw dropped in surprise, and he even leaned out of his lodge to watch her retreating back. He'd never seen Professor Lewis in the company of a woman before.

The three of them entered the senior common room of Magdalen College. Joy could see at once that this party was *not*, as Jack had termed it, "nothing of any importance." The president's annual Christmas cocktail party for the professors and their wives was in fact one of the most important social events of the academic year. The large common room, wood-paneled, hung with old portraits in large gilded frames, was filled with dons; the married ones had brought their wives, quiet creatures dressed in black, brown, or gray dresses, and all wearing modest pearl chokers at their throats. Young or old, the wives tended to look and act the same, pale shadows of their illustrious husbands.

Jack helped Joy off with her coat. All around them conversation stopped, as partygoers stared at the strange woman who'd come in with Jack Lewis. They saw a slender, dark-haired, attractive woman in a fashionable red dress that stood out like a stop sign in this sober gathering. Who in the world could this strange woman be?

"Come and meet the college president," said Jack, mindful that every eye in the room seemed to be on him and Joy, and that every academic brain was speculating wildly. He knew exactly what they were thinking. Jack Lewis with a woman! A much younger woman in a red dress! He felt foolish that he was so pleased about Joy's good looks, especially tonight in her party dress, and with her hair arranged so becomingly. He knew that the subject of Jack Lewis and a woman would be brought up and thoroughly chewed over in the senior common room some night soon, over glasses of port, when he himself was absent.

"Where on earth did he find her?" demanded Christopher Riley, cornering Warnie. Christopher absolutely detested not being in on things, or being among the last to know something. And Jack Lewis, sly dog that he was, had not let drop that this American of his was such a pretty woman. Riley had pictured her as some bovine clubwoman type, with a tight permanent smile and bad teeth. Not this stunner.

"She wrote to him," answered Warnie.

"Ah, a pen pal." Riley's cultured voice dripped with sarcasm. He was literally burning with curiosity.

A waiter passed by them carrying a tray of drinks. "There she blows!" cried Warnie, and set off in hot pursuit. He wanted a drink badly, but more than that he wanted to get away from Christopher Riley and Christopher's acid wit and biting questions.

Riley, not willing to let the matter rest until he had solved the mystery of Jack's pretty houseguest, followed his nose through the crowd in the room until he fetched up at the little group surrounding Jack and Joy.

"So this is your first trip to England, Mrs. Gresham?" asked the college chaplain, Harry Harrington.

"Yes, my first," smiled Joy. "But I've wanted to come for a long time."

"What brings you to England, Mrs. Gresham?" Nick Farrell wanted to know.

"Well, I've been working on a book . . . and . . . well . . . I was hoping to get a publisher interested over here." It was unlike Joy to hesitate, and it flickered across Lewis's mind to wonder why.

"Ah, there you are, Christopher," called Jack. Joy looked over to see a tall, dark, and rather sardonic-looking man approaching them, his eyes fixed firmly on her.

"Yes, Jack, here I am." Riley kept looking pointedly at Joy, as if demanding an explanation of her very existence.

"Let me introduce you to Mrs. Joy Gresham. Professor Christopher Riley."

"Professor Riley." Joy nodded coolly.

"How do you do?" Riley's smile was so fixed it was positively unnerving. There was an air of tension around him always, as though he were an unexploded bomb. Joy sensed it, and determined to keep a distance between them.

"So," the chaplain broke into the awkward silence, "what success have you had with your book?"

"To be honest, it isn't ready to show to anyone yet," she answered frankly.

"Oh, you mustn't let that stop you, Mrs. Gresham," Christopher Riley purred. "It doesn't stop Jack."

"I'm sorry?" Joy's eyes widened. Could she have possibly heard him correctly?

"I am right in assuming that you are from the United States of America?"

"Yes, I am."

"Then perhaps you can satisfy my curiosity on a related matter," continued Christopher Riley smoothly. "I had always understood Americans to be hard-riding, tough-talking, no-nonsense sort of people, and yet Jack tells me his children's stories sell very well over there. Who can be buying them?"

"We're not all cowboys, Professor Riley," said Joy coldly. "Have you read any of Jack's children's books?"

"Jack has read excerpts aloud to me. It is one of his tests of friendship."

Tests? *Tests!* Who did this man think he was, criticizing C. S. Lewis's masterpieces? "I think they're magical," Joy said.

Riley turned to Jack, but his smile remained fixed and sarcastic. "Congratulations, Jack. You seem to have found a soul mate."

"I thought you believed we didn't have souls, Christopher," Unruffled, Lewis smiles at his old antagonist.

"Well, now, you see, I regard the soul as an essentially feminine accessory. *Anima*. Quite different from *animus*, the male variant. This is how I explain the otherwise puzzling difference between the sexes. Where men have intellect, women have soul."

Joy Gresham's eyebrow flew up, which Lewis already had come to recognize as a danger signal. Her dark gray eyes flashed sparks. "Professor Riley," she said slowly, "as you say, I'm from the United States, and different cultures have different modes of discourse. I need a little guidance here. Are you being offensive, or merely stupid?"

Oh, my God, I've done it again! thought Joy, appalled. *I opened my big mouth and embarrassed Jack, right here in his college.* Even so, she wasn't sorry, she was rather glad she'd put the male chauvinist snob in his place. And, to judge from the fact that Christopher Riley stood there speechless, his mouth just opening and closing and nothing coming out, in his place was just where she'd put him.

And, if the gleam in Jack Lewis's eye was to be believed, he was far less embarrassed than proud of her. Joy Gresham had accomplished what C. S. Lewis never could; she had shut Christopher Riley up.

The attic at The Kilns—especially the tall wooden wardrobe in the far corner—held a strong fascination for Douglas Gresham. Although his rational senses didn't allow him to actually believe that it was the gateway to the wonderworld of Narnia, part of him, the deepest part, the part most attuned to magical possibilities, nevertheless kept asking "What if?"

Of the three novels published so far in Lewis's seven-volume series *The Chronicles of Narnia*, Douglas's favorite was the first, *The Lion, the Witch and the Wardrobe*. In it, a kindly professor lives in a big old house in the country, and during the war he takes in a group of children evacuees, who are fleeing German bombs. One rainy day, playing hide-and-seek, Lucy runs to hide in a large wardrobe, which is in reality the gateway to the fantasy world of Narnia. She is followed by the other children, and in Narnia they meet Asian, the powerful and good talking lion, and many otherworldly creatures, both powerfully good and powerfully evil.

Now, here was Douglas, in the country, in the house of a kindly old professor, who was also the author of his favorite book. What if the wardrobe in the real author's real home was the real wardrobe in the book? Lewis's novel had made a deep and lasting impression on Douglas. Last time they were here, it was only for afternoon tea, and Douglas, a curious child, had been given no time to explore. But now that they were here for several days, for Christmas, his fascination—and his secret hopes—drew him up to the attic. And to the wardrobe.

On Christmas morning, after they had all returned from church and the carol singing in the Magdalen College chapel, Douglas tackled the attic. He made his way through the old trunks and boxes, past dress forms and cricket bats, until he was standing in front of the wardrobe. He reached his hand out and touched it tentatively. It was wood; it looked and felt like wood; it didn't move. He opened it and looked inside. Coats. One or two fur coats as in *The Lion, the Witch and the Wardrobe,* but most of them were ordinary everyday woolen coats. A couple of boys' coats, more than forty years old and sadly out of style. Warnie's old military greatcoat, too small to fit the major now. A powerful smell of mothballs came from the closet, making Douglas wrinkle his nose.

But behind the coats—what? In *The Lion, the Witch and the Wardrobe,* if you pushed your way through to the back of the wardrobe, behind the fur coats you would find the gate to the magical realm of Narnia. Douglas reached his hands through the coats, feeling for the back, and there it was—the back of the wardrobe. Just another solid wooden wall. No magic. *I knew that,* thought Douglas, but bitter disillusion brought tears to his eyes.

"It stood in our nursery when we were children," said Jack quietly. He was standing in the attic doorway, watching Douglas with sympathy. He understood the boy's disappointment; he was beginning to feel a kinship with the quiet, bookish, imaginative child who believed in magic. It was surprising to him, because, as his fellow don Rupert Parrish had pointed out, Jack Lewis didn't know any children.

"If you don't need it anymore, you should throw it away," Douglas muttered angrily.

Jack understood the boy's resentment; the mundane old nursery wardrobe must be a big disappointment to a child who was hoping for magic. "I'm not very good at throwing things away, you see." He waved a hand at the piles of abandoned possessions that were still kept faithfully in storage.

"We don't have an attic at home."

"You wish you were home, don't you?" There was no mistaking the wistfulness in Douglas's expression.

"We always have a turkey for Christmas at home."

"We'll be having a turkey here," Jack pointed out.

Douglas brightened a little. "With cranberry sauce?" he asked hopefully.

"Ah." That meant no.

"My dad loves cranberry sauce."

Evidently, the boy's thoughts were much involved with his father, and Jack realized that the sadness he sensed in Douglas was a part of it. He didn't know what to say.

"Does he?"

"And snow." Douglas had expected snow for Christmas; in America they almost always had snow. Here in England all they had was mud. Cold houses and mud. And no cranberry sauce. He wanted to go home.

"Who do you look like most, your mother or your father?" asked Jack, curious, but also to change the subject.

Douglas covered the upper half of his face with his hands. "This is Mom." And Jack could see the resemblance to Joy—the full mouth, the vulnerable set of the lips, the pointed chin. Then the boy covered the lower half, exposing only the eyes and the brow. "This is Dad."

The boy's steady gaze was disconcerting to Lewis. "But Dad's kind of noisy, and I'm not," said Douglas thoughtfully.

"What kind of noisy?"

"Like, shouting. I hate shouting."

"Me, too," Jack agreed.

Douglas closed the doors of the wardrobe. "I

knew it was just an old wardrobe." But he couldn't hide the disillusion in his voice. He'd been hoping for the fantasy gateway to Narnia, but all he got was old coats.

Together, the man and the boy left the unmagical attic.

Later, as the housekeeper was preparing the Christmas turkey, Lewis poked his head into the kitchen. "We wouldn't happen to have any cranberry sauce, Mrs. Young, would we?"

"Cranberry sauce? What's that?" Her plump perspiring features crinkled in a frown.

Jack shrugged, embarrassed. "My guess is it's a sauce made with cranberries."

As though she didn't have enough to do, with all these guests! "Well, Mr. Lewis," she told him crossly, "if you can find me some cranberries, I'll sauce 'em."

They sat down to Christmas dinner at four o'clock on the dot, because Mrs. Young wanted to get home to her own family. There was a fire burning brightly in the dining room hearth, and garlands made of colorful paper rings were strung over the mantelpiece, which exhibited a large number of Christmas cards, most of them for Jack. Some of the cards came from the far corners of the world, from his fans and his correspondents, from his publishers and colleagues.

There was wine with dinner, and Warnie had already begun on the bottle. He and Douglas picked their Christmas crackers up from beside their plates, broke the golden seals, and pulled them open with a loud crack. They were wearing the paper party hats they'd found inside. Jack, of course, wore no fancy hat; it would be impossible to imagine him in one. Joy, not wishing to abandon her host as the only one without a paper hat, had left hers inside the cracker, but secretly she wanted to put the silly thing on.

Mrs. Young, her face covered with drops of perspiration, carried the turkey in from the kitchen and set it down. She returned with the boiled vegetables—potatoes and sprouts and olive-colored green peas as hard as buckshot—and put the bowls on the table. Then she returned for one last trip from the kitchen, putting a jar of raspberry jam and a jam spoon down next to Douglas. So much for cranberry sauce. But she'd done her best.

Jack carved the bird, which was not difficult, because the turkey was so well done it virtually fell off the bone. He filled a plate with meat and vegetables, and handed it to Joy. The second plateful went to Douglas, who sat regarding it in mingled horror and dismay. Taking up the jar of jam, Joy passed it over to her son.

100

Joy couldn't help but recognize the look on Douglas's face. She leaned over to him. "Just eat it," she whispered. Reluctantly, Douglas raised his fork to his lips and took a bite. The tough, shredded turkey was very different from the crisp roasted bird he was used to, and the boy began to chew it with difficulty.

"And we should raise a glass to your husband, Joy," smiled Jack Lewis.

"Sure, why not?" She lifted her glass. "To Bill." Warnie and Jack lifted their wineglasses in the toast, and Douglas held up his glass of warm orange squash. "To Bill!" "To Dad!" They all drank the toast, Warnie draining his glass and filling it up again immediately. Jack, as usual, drank very little.

"Can you telephone to America?" Douglas asked suddenly.

"No, no," Joy put in sharply. "We'll be home soon enough."

"You're very welcome if you want," Jack said, misunderstanding.

"I do want." The boy's eyes were eager.

"It's far too expensive, Douglas." Joy turned to Jack, her face strained. "He's only excited by the novelty of it."

"I am not!" Douglas cried, and his lips trembled. "I want to talk to Dad."

"Well you can't," snapped Joy. "And that's that."

Her strictness seemed to Jack inexplicable, very much at odds with Joy's usual loving behavior to her son. An awkward silence fell.

Warnie saved the day without even being aware of it. He was by now at least half potted, and getting tipsier by the minute. "Beastly things, telephones," he said thickly. "Ring-ring-ring! Stop what you're doing! Get up! Hurry hurry! Ring-ring-ring! No manners at all."

Warnie's outburst had them all laughing, including Warnie himself, and the strange tension of the moment passed.

After the meal, there were carols broadcast over the wireless, and they exchanged their modest Christmas gifts. Jack gave his brother a carved walking stick, sturdier and more handsome than his old one, and received in exchange a decent pair of woolen gloves. For Joy and Douglas, there were signed copies of C. S. Lewis books from Jack, and scarves from Warnie. The scarves occasioned a round of laughter, because they were almost exactly what Joy and Douglas had brought as gifts for Warnie and Jack Lewis.

"Great minds, eh?" said Warnie.

"You bet," smiled Joy.

After the gifts were opened, Warnie took himself off to his bedroom to sleep off the heavy meal and the wine, and Joy went upstairs soon afterward to tuck Douglas into bed. It had been a long day and, except for that moment of unpleasantness at the dinner table, a happy one.

Especially memorable was the carol singing by the magnificent Oxford choir, like a chorus of angels announcing the great miracle of Christ's birth. Joy was tickled to see C. S. Lewis in his don's robes, standing with the other dons in their appointed places, while she and Douglas and Warnie occupied seats in the visitors' pews. She was moved by the singing, and by the feeling of exaltation she got from the Church of England Christmas service set in the wonderful old Gothic chapel, many centuries old, and the fragmented light that poured through the magnificent stained-glass windows, spreading colors like precious gems over the intricately carved pews. Candles burned, and the choristers in their snowy gowns gleamed like angels.

When she came downstairs again, Joy found Jack sitting alone in an armchair in the drawing room, which was still littered with Christmas wrappings.

"All well?" he asked.

"All well," Joy smiled. "Douglas never makes a fuss about going to bed."

"He appears never to make a fuss about anything. Except telephones, perhaps."

Jack's words were mild, but Joy sensed a clear reproach. He thought she had been too hard on the boy, had snatched away an opportunity for Douglas to be happy, and all for no good reason. Just an arbitrary display of power. "Right," she said, her cheeks burning.

"Warnie has taken himself off to bed, too. Sometimes he overdoes it a little. I expect you noticed."

"Yes." Joy nodded. "I know the signs."

"There are signs, are there? Poor Warnie." Jack sighed.

"You know, don't you?" Joy asked suddenly.

Her words took Jack Lewis by surprise. "Know what?"

"You must think I'm not much of a mother, someone who won't let her son phone his father on Christmas Day."

Now it was Lewis's turn to be embarrassed. "Not at all—it's none of my—"

"It just isn't the way it looks, that's all," cut in Joy. She couldn't meet his eyes and kept hers on the view outside the drawing room window. She appeared to be close to tears, and struggling mightily with herself to regain her composure. Jack sat watching her, once again not knowing what to say.

"Thank you for not asking," said Joy.

"Not asking what?"

" 'What's this woman doing chasing around England without her husband?' " It was a good imitation of a prude, and almost word for word Warnie's criticism, and no doubt the criticism of others as well.

"Ah. That." Jack didn't bother to deny that the subject had crossed his mind.

"I'm running away. Always a mistake, isn't it? You have to face things in the end." She stood up abruptly and walked to the fireplace on the far side of the room, keeping her face turned away so that Jack Lewis wouldn't see the pain in her eyes or the trembling of her lips.

"I left home because Bill fell in love with another woman," she said bitterly. "Bill takes the romantic view; if you love someone, you marry them. I'm Number Two. He wants me to give him a divorce, so he can marry Number Three."

"I see."

"This is what's called breathing space." She paused a moment, then the truth came pouring out of Joy Gresham against her will. "Bill's an alcoholic, he's compulsively unfaithful, he's sometimes violent, and I guess I haven't loved him in years."

"Violent?" asked Lewis, concern for her suddenly washing over him.

Joy nodded, exhausted. Her face was pinched and small, and Jack could see the lines etched around her mouth. "Only when he's drunk. He doesn't know what he's doing. He's worn me out, that's the truth of it. The only thing that's new is that now he wants a divorce."

"I had no idea," Jack said slowly and truthfully. He was at a loss; what should he do? Pat her shoulder? Take her hand? He was certain that Joy didn't want to be touched at this moment, and for that he was grateful. He was in over his head here, trying to keep afloat in a flood of personal revelation and raw emotion. But everything was clearer to him now, Joy Gresham's occasionally overbright vivacity, and the sadness in her little boy's eyes. Douglas's dislike of noise and shouting. The boy must have heard considerable noise and shouting.

Joy smiled wanly. "I'm sorry to burden you with all this. It's not your problem. Don't worry. I'll be all right. I always have been."

Troubled, Jack said nothing.

On the day after Christmas, Joy Gresham and her son returned to London. It was once again time for goodbyes. Their visit had been brief, yet fraught with revelations, and dangers to all of them. They had avoided the pitfalls; they were still all friends. At least that was something. At the end of the year, they'd be sailing back to America, and presumably Joy and Jack would return to being pen pals.

"Goodbye, Warnie," smiled Joy as the suitcases were put into the taxi's boot. "Thank you for putting up with us."

"Not at all. We shall miss you," said Warnie munificently.

"Goodbye, Jack." She smiled at him warmly, but her eyes held sadness.

"Goodbye, then, Joy." As usual, Lewis felt awkward around Joy Gresham. Jack looked around for Douglas, to say goodbye, but the boy was already sitting in the taxi, his face somber. For him, goodbye was an occasion of loss; the child hated goodbyes. Jack Lewis understood that, because he felt the same way himself. His eyes met Douglas's, and each gave a small but significant nod of the head.

The taxi drove off to the station. Jack turned to his brother. "That's that, Warnie."

"Right, Jack." But Warnie didn't believe a word of it. As far as he could tell, that was very far from that.

FIVE

Surprised by Joy

After Joy Gresham sailed back to the United States, an unexpected silence fell between them. Jack was certain he'd be hearing from her any day, and eagerly scanned every morning's and afternoon's post for the tissue-thin blue airmail envelope, that familiar handwriting. Every day, dozens of letters arrived for him from all over the globe, but not one of them was from Joy. January gave way to February, Christmas was only a fading memory, and still no word from Joy. Jack Lewis's most faithful correspondent had apparently deserted him, and he had no idea why. Although he would not have admitted it, even to himself, he felt abandoned.

Because Joy wasn't writing to him, Jack couldn't bring himself to write to her, deeming it intrusive. He missed the wit and sparkle of her letters; he missed the challenges she presented to his way of thinking, the intellectual give-and-take that had developed between them. It was as though a window had opened into his life, bringing with it drafts of fresh, invigorating air. Now that window was shut again. It seemed to Lewis that an enjoyable conversation had been abruptly and mysteriously broken off. But it was more than that, and he dared not own up to it.

It was Warnie who, in his customary simple and direct way, put it into words. One day, "You miss her, don't you?" Warnie asked sympathetically. He'd just brought the morning post into the study where Jack was working, and it pained him to watch his brother drop what he was doing and rifle through the letters with such expectation, and to see the expectation die away in disappointment.

"Things are quieter now." Jack gave a small shrug, reticent as always.

Warnie was just beginning to realize how much Joy's conversations with Jack had meant to Jack. She was a stimulating woman, always bubbling with ideas, expressing them with vivacity and humor. The more outrageous the ideas, the more vigorously she defended them. Joy was more than a match for the eminent C. S. Lewis, who counted verbal sparring with a person of high intelligence one of the greatest pleasures of life. Up to now, all of his intellectual jousts had been with men, mostly other writers and fellows of Magdalen College. Joy was the first woman ever to penetrate those defenses and enter the castle. "I'm not much of a talker," Warnie apologized.

"One of your many virtues, Warnie," Jack replied with fondness.

"Is she coming back?"

Lewis shook his head. "No, no." He looked up from his work and smiled at his brother. "I haven't really thanked you, Warnie."

"What for?"

"You've been very tolerant, very considerate." Many words lay unspoken between them. But Warnie understood, because he knew his brother so well.

"Any friend of yours, Jack."

"I know."

He's changed, Warnie thought sadly. *He doesn't realize it, but he's not the same man he was before Joy Gresham came*. But Warnie Lewis wasn't much of a talker, so he said nothing. Better that way, perhaps.

Outside the bookshop windows, the late February rain poured steadily down in a gray curtain. A parade of black umbrellas went by, with long rivulets of water streaming down the cloth, and forming new puddles on the High Street. Inside

Blackwell's, one of England's—if not the world's—greatest bookstores, C. S. Lewis was autographing copies of his books.

This was not one of his favorite occupations, this sitting in one place and smiling at a lineup of strangers and signing his name again and again, but it made Macmillan, his publisher, happy. And, because both Blackwell's and C. S. Lewis helped to make Oxford famous, and because Blackwell's always put a handsome display of Lewis's latest work in their window, and sold so many copies of this local celebrity's books, Jack knew he was obligated to Blackwell's, too.

"Thank you so much, Mr. Lewis." An elderly lady clasped her newly signed copy of *Mere Christianity* to her bosom, as though it were a treasure.

The next in line was a young boy. For a moment, Lewis was reminded of Douglas Gresham, and he felt a sudden pang. "Thank you, sir," the lad said, holding out his copy of *The Magician's Nephew*. It was C. S. Lewis's newest work, the sixth volume in the Narnia series, and already a bestseller. "Good, good," Lewis smiled, signing the book with a flourish.

As he handed it back, Lewis happened to look across the store, and spotted Peter Whistler, from his romantic poetry course, browsing in the far stacks. The student's strange rebel nature was of

111

more than passing interest to Jack, so he watched
him for a minute as the young man pored over the
titles on the shelf. Then, with a shock of surprise,
Lewis saw Whistler select a volume and slip it into
his bookbag. Surely, he was going to pay for it! But,
as he continued to watch from a distance, Whistler
left the shop without paying. *He's stolen that book!*
thought Lewis in dismay, but he said nothing, only
turned his attention back to the next person in the
autographing line. Yet he knew that there was
something he himself ought to be doing about it.

The following day was a speaking engagement in
the Midlands, where once again he delivered his
words on God's intentions toward the pain of humanity, the lecture which was the most beloved of
his audiences.

"I'm not sure that God particularly wants us to
be happy. He wants us to be able to love, and be
loved. He wants us to grow up. We think our
childish toys bring us all the happiness there is,
and our nursery is the whole wide world. Something must drive us out of the nursery, to the world
of others. Isn't that something . . . suffering?"

Once again, a standing ovation. Some people
even had tears in their eyes. But Lewis's thoughts
were not on his listeners or even on his own words,
they were on Peter Whistler. Surely, there was

somebody in need of help. As soon as he returned to Oxford, he went to look for the boy.

He knew that Whistler lived in college rooms somewhere at Magdalen. The undergraduate rooms were in the quads, off the cloistered walks, and up narrow staircases. There were several rooms to one entrance, with numerous entrances opening onto the cloister walkway. So he went from doorway to doorway, reading the names painted on the walls, until he found Whistler. The stairs were narrow and dark, and it was a long climb to the top. Outside Whistler's door, Lewis hesitated. Did he have a right to be here? No, the better question was, did he have a right *not* to be here? No, that he did not. He knocked on the heavy oak door, waited a moment, then knocked again, this time more loudly.

After a moment, the door opened, and Whistler, even more unkempt than usual, peered out. "I hope you don't mind," Lewis said quietly.

"Come in." Reluctantly, the boy opened the door and Lewis entered. The room was icy cold and very untidy, not only because of the customary under-graduate clutter, but also because of the piles of books that were everywhere. Books stood on the shelves, and were stacked haphazardly on the floor, on the single chair, on the window seat. Books on top of books on top of books. Whistler said nothing, but stood with a resentful expression on his face, waiting to learn why Professor C. S. Lewis was here, in his room.

Lewis decided it was better to come right to the point. "I happened to be in Blackwell's the other day. I saw you . . . borrow . . . a book."

"Steal. I stole it," Whistler admitted at once. He waved one arm around, in an inclusive gesture. "Most of these books are stolen. Why not? They're written to be read. At least I *read* them, which is more than most people do."

"You read books differently from the rest of us, do you?" Lewis was nettled by the young man's arrogance, yet curious. Of all the things one could steal, books were surely among the most unusual.

"Yes, I do." The young man nodded his head venemently. His thin cheeks were a dull red, and his eyes shone with a feverish brightness. As he spoke, his North Country accent became even more pronounced. "I read at night, so nothing breaks my concentration. All night, sometimes. When I start a new book, my hands are shaking, my eyes are jumping ahead. Does the writer feel the way I've felt? Does he see what I see? Yes, that's good, that's true. No, he's cheating, he's ducking it. Ah, wait, that may be so—yes, yes, he's seen it, too! My father used to say—he's a teacher, like you—no, no, not like you, only a village schoolmaster—what was it you asked me? How do I read? Sometimes I shout at the book, or I kiss the page, or I cry. . . ."

Whistler broke off, conscious that he was no longer making any sense, waiting for the celebrated scholar, the eminent author and lecturer C. S. Lewis to mock at him or reproach him, to use his superiority as a weapon against him.

But Lewis did none of these things. He had listened with strong interest to every word. Now he only asked mildly, "What was it your father used to say?"

" 'We read to know we're not alone.' "

The simple words struck Lewis. What a wonderful truth, he thought. We read to know we're not alone. And how well Peter Whistler had learned it! His opinion of his student underwent a profound change. "Would it help if I made you a small loan?" he asked quietly.

"I expect it would, if I wanted to be helped." Whistler spoke dismissively, but just as quietly.

"I see. Goodbye." Lewis's hand dropped to his side. He'd been rebuffed; his help was not wanted here. There seemed nothing more to say. At least now he understood the boy better. And had felt, for the first time, some understanding of his tortured rebelliousness. Whistler, the fallen angel.

No doubt his struggle on earth would be a difficult one.

Jack looked up from the notes he was taking and sighed. "I've always found this a trying time of the year," he said to Christopher Riley, who sat across from him at the same library table in the reading room of Radcliffe Camera. The place had a subterranean, almost tomblike feel to it, reinforced by the tall bookstacks that rose all up around them, like dolmens.

Riley didn't look up from the scholarly periodical he was reading. The vast university library was silent and solemn, and readers rarely spoke here. "Trying to do what, Jack?"

Jack's voice held a tinge of sadness. "The leaves not yet out. Mud everywhere you go. The frosty mornings gone, the sunny mornings not yet come. Give me blizzards and frozen pipes, but not this morning time. Not this waiting room of a world. Tell me something, Christopher. How can I put this? Would you say that you were content?"

Putting his book down, Riley gave his full attention to the question. "I am as I am. The world is at it is. My contentment or otherwise has very little to do with it."

"You don't ever feel a sense of waste?" asked Lewis in a low tone.

Riley raised his eyebrow, and a sardonic answer formed on his lips. But the expression on Jack's face precluded sarcasm. For the first time, Christopher felt that Jack Lewis was reaching out to him in a personal way, not as a colleague but as a friend, and that there was something more on Jack's mind than scholarly speculation.

"Of course," he said quietly, and they exchanged silent glances. Then both men returned to their work and there was silence in the Radcliffe library once again.

In early March of 1954, C. S. Lewis found himself again in London addressing an attentive group of Christian women, all of whom had paid three shillings to hear him. Lewis delivered his pet lecture on human suffering, which by now was so ingrained in his memory that he needed no notes. If you woke him up at three in the morning and primed him with the first two words, Jack Lewis could deliver the entire lecture without opening his eyes. But he had no compunctions about giving it once again; people seemed to love it, to respond to it, and to derive real comfort from it.

"Could it be precisely because God loves us that he makes us the gift of suffering? We're like blocks of stone, out of which the sculptor carves the forms of men. The blows of his chisel, which hurt us so much, are what make us perfect." He stopped, silent, while a roar of applause rose to deafen him.

Immediately afterward, a knot of women formed around him, to worship and to praise. The chairwoman tried to hold them back, but the women pressed forward, eager for a word, a look, an acknowledgement of some kind.

"Mr. Lewis, what can I say?"

"Mr. Lewis, if you have a moment—"

"Mr. Lewis, I just had to come up and say thank you—"

"Mr. Lewis, I don't like to bother you—" said another, fully intent on bothering him.

The chairwoman interposed her authority between the celebrity and his admirers. "I'm sure what Mr. Lewis would like now is a cup of tea," she said firmly.

Yes, a cup of tea was precisely what Mr. Lewis wanted, what he'd kill for. The chairwoman bustled off, and the large hall began to clear, most people leaving, and a small cluster of diehards waiting to approach the speaker after his tea. Suddenly, Jack Lewis caught a glimpse of a small figure sitting alone, a dark-haired woman with an oval face that was a hammer blow to his heart. It was, astoundingly and after all these months, after he was sure he'd never see her again in this life, Joy Gresham.

Then, in the departing crowd, she was lost to view.

"Why don't I go on ahead and make sure the tea's ready?" asked the chairwoman, pleased with her own efficiency.

"Do. Yes. Thank you," Jack said gratefully. Go to Ceylon and pick the leaves. Go to Jamaica and cut the sugar. Go to Devon and milk the cow. Only—whatever you do—don't come back soon. In a daze, he pushed his way down the few steps from the stage and through the auditorium, shaking hands and receiving congratulations as he made his way toward the place where Joy had been. Like Moses through the Rea Sea, Jack Lewis crossed dry-shod and stood at last in front of Joy Gresham.

She was even prettier than he remembered, unless it was only in contrast to the drab middle-aged hens who made up most of his audience today. But no, there was a freshness in her cheeks and a sparkle in her fine eyes that lit up her entire being.

"Hello, Jack."

"What are you doing here?" It was a rude thing to say, not even a hello first, but Jack was unaware of his words.

"I came to hear your talk," she said simply.

"Yes, but . . ."

"What am I doing in London?" Joy interrupted, and the familiar mischievous gleam flashed in her

119

eyes. "I live here now. What have I done with Bill? We're divorced. What have I done with Douglas? He's in London with me."

Warnie was right. He had missed her. It was borne in on him all at once how much he missed her—her American bluntness and truthfulness, her innate disdain for pretension and lying, the expression in her dark gray eyes and around her full mouth. "Why didn't you write?" demanded Lewis.

"What for? To ask permission?" The corners of Joy's lips twitched as she surpressed a smile.

"No, no . . ." he took her literally.

"Do you mind?" Joy tilted her head to look up at Jack and her eyes sought his.

"Me? No. Why should I mind?"

"That's all right, then."

"I really am very . . . very surprised to see you, you know."

Joy had never seen Jack Lewis be anything but perfectly articulate. This slight stammer, the hesitation was new to her. Dared she find it flattering?

"I wasn't dead. I was only in America."

"Yes, of course. But, you see, I've been thinking about . . . I've been thinking about you."

He was thinking about me, thought Joy with pleasure, and she wasn't certain which pleasure was the greater, the fact that Jack Lewis had her in his

120

thoughts or the fact that he was able to confess it to her.

"Can I be of any assistance?" The chairwoman had grown tired of waiting for Lewis in the committee room and had come to find him.

"I'm just talking to my friend," he said, ignoring her. "I was thinking about you," he told Joy. "And, suddenly, there you were."

"Here I am," Joy laughed. "Present tense. Present, and tense."

"I'm sorry, but the committee is waiting to entertain Mr. Lewis," insisted the chairwoman in a proprietary way. She gave Joy a grimace with bared teeth, a fixed smile without recognition—just another woman annoying their precious guest.

"Let me know where you are," Jack said as the committeewoman hauled him off for his tea. He cast one helpless longing glance back at Joy, left alone in the now empty auditorium.

Joy watched until Jack Lewis had disappeared from view. Then she picked up her purse and gloves and left the auditorium.

"So she's settled here for good, has she?" asked Warnie casually from his desk chair across the study. He didn't look up from the *Times* crossword.

"For the foreseeable future." Jack continued

correcting the set of galleys which had arrived by post from his publisher this morning.

"With the boy?"

"Yes."

"Will you be seeing much of her?" Although Warnie's tone didn't change, it was in fact a loaded question.

"Not much, I shouldn't think," Jack replied casually. "I may look in when I'm next in London."

C. S. Lewis's schedule was always a busy one; he was so much in demand that it was no wonder he found himself in London fairly regularly, to lecture or to deliver another of his radio talks. But, on leaving BBC House, instead of rushing for the Oxford train as he almost always did, Lewis headed for the Underground and took the Northern Line to the Finchley tube station. Once outside the station, he began to walk.

Joy Gresham's flat was in a small cul-de-sac off the Finchley Road, in one of those semidetached chimney-pot houses that line the side streets of North London. To Jack's eye, the street was grimy and depressing. There were no front gardens, no window boxes, not even a tree to break the monotony of soot-begrimed brick. While not a slum, the street where Joy Gresham lived spoke of near-poverty, of cheese-paring to make do, of low rents and frequent despair.

Yet Joy's basement flat spoke not of despair but of hope. It was shiningly clean and cheerful, with colorful contemporary artist prints hanging unframed on the walls, and books everywhere, and small bunches of flowers that Joy had picked up cheaply at a stall by the tube station, "hyacinths to feed the soul," as the poet wrote. In Joy's flat the kettle whistled a welcome, and tea was served in crockery mugs that were brightly colored. Best of all, there was Joy, smiling a hello.

Jack Lewis kept on finding his way to London fairly often after that first visit. He always had a good excuse for going—a broadcast, a visit to Macmillan, his publisher, some research at the library of the British Museum, as though Oxford's Bodleian and Camera Radcliffe libraries didn't hold all the book-wisdom of the universe, or to give a lecture here or a reading there—but Warnie wasn't fooled. He was well aware that Jack went to London to see Joy Gresham.

Only Jack himself was fooled. But he managed to integrate Joy and Douglas into his life with almost no trouble to himself. The little flat off the Finchley Road was only a pleasant place to visit for a warm welcome, good company, and excellent conversation. He and Joy argued happily about everything—literature, music, politics, the state of the world—everything except religion. There, they were in total agreement, both possessing the fervor of the converted.

The three of them—Jack, Joy, and Douglas—often had an early dinner together, so that Jack could make the last train back to Oxford. Sometimes Joy cooked, mostly casseroles, nourishing and cheap. Sometimes Jack treated them all to curry in an Indian restaurant in the Finchley Road. Sometimes, to please Douglas with his favorite meal, Jack brought in a large package of fried plaice and chips, from the nearby fish and chips shop. But whatever they ate, they ate with laughter and washed down with affection.

One day in late spring, when all of England except, it seemed, Joy Gresham's street, had finally burst into bloom, Jack Lewis arrived at Joy's flat early in the afternoon. As usual, he stopped before ringing the bell and looked into the windows of the basement flat, hoping to be able to see Joy before she saw him. He enjoyed watching her go about the most mundane tasks unaware that he was peeping at her.

Although Joy hadn't expected him so early, she was happy to see Jack. She prepared a light lunch which they ate together, and, when Joy had to leave to pick up Douglas from school, Jack took her by surprise by announcing that he would come along with her. This was a first.

The two arrived just as the little inexpensive private school was letting out for the afternoon. A stream of children came running happily out of the building, bare-kneed, caps on their heads, crests on their blazers, which were piped in the school colors. They were all boys, and Douglas was among them, looking very different from the American Douglas Gresham who had arrived at The Kilns a couple of years ago, wearing a plaid wool jacket and a checked wool cap with earflaps. Now it was impossible to tell him from the other boys.

Joy watched the boys running happily out of the school, and smiled with amusement. Just about every grade school in the States was coeducational, girls and boys together. Here in England if was so different. "You really go in for segregation of the sexes here, don't you?"

Lewis laughed. "Did you know that in Oxford dons weren't even allowed to be married until the 1880s? You'll still find plenty of dons who believe that family life is the ruin of a fine mind."

"Including you?" Joy cast a sideways glance at Jack.

"How would I know? I've never been married."

"Do you ever get asked why?"

"Sometimes," Jack admitted. "But what monstrous arrogance! To assume that your own way of life is normal, and all other ways are aberrations

125

that need explaining!" His voice rose in indignation.

"I'm glad now I didn't ask." Joy's gray eyes danced, and the corners of her full lips twitched in a little smile.

Late spring, 1956. As Jack had promised Warnie, things at The Kilns continued as they always had, in a quiet and even tenor, with day following day and season following season. Jack Lewis's time went on being divided between Oxford and London; his work was going very well indeed. He had completed the seventh and last volume in *The Chronicles of Narnia,* a novel called *The Last Battle.* He was putting together a collection of his *Reflections on the Psalms,* and making notes on science and theology for a book he was thinking of titling *Shall We Lose God in Outer Space?.*

By now the way to Joy Gresham's basement flat was a very familiar one. A home away from home, as Jack liked to think of it. His relationship with Joy was for him as comfortable as old slippers, warm and friendly and free from tension. Although she continued to refuse to accept money from him, Jack knew she was living on very little. Her ex-husband could send her only sixty dollars a month, which translated into less than fifteen pounds. So every time he came, instead of bringing only a bunch of flowers or a bottle of wine, Jack also arrived with a packet of chops, or a bag of groceries, or fresh butter and eggs from an Oxfordshire farm.

And, almost always, he brought a new book along for Douglas. Books were the necessities of Douglas's life; he devoured them as other boys devoured sweets. Jack had become very fond of the boy; more and more, the quiet and introspective, sensitive Douglas reminded Jack Lewis of himself as a lad.

"It's sweet of you to come and see me, Jack." Joy's smile was unusually bright this evening. "I know how busy you are."

"Not at all. I look forward to my outings to London." Lewis took his coat off and hung it in the front closet. He felt totally at ease here. "You must come and visit us in Oxford one day."

Joy nodded. "Maybe when Douglas gets out of school. I'd like to see Warnie again. Do remember me to him, and tell him I promise I won't turn into a nuisance."

"Why should you turn into a nuisance?"

"Oh, come on, Jack," said Joy impatiently. "I don't have to explain."

"Explain what?" Joy was regarding him so oddly, and with such intensity that Jack felt the first stirrings of alarm. "Why are you looking at me like that?" he asked.

"Like what?"

"As if I'm lying to you. Why should I lie to you? I mean what I say."

"I know that," she stated flatly. "But you don't say it all, do you?"

Lewis hesitated, feeling anxiety lying like a lump in his chest. He'd been certain that this arrangement between them was as comfortable for Joy as it was for himself. Was Joy trying to get him to say something he didn't want to, to commit himself in some way beyond the first great commitment of friendship? "One can't say it all. It would take too long."

At that moment, Douglas appeared in the doorway, wearing pajamas and holding a book. "Finished your chapter, dear?" Joy asked.

"Almost. Very nearly." He had finished, of course, but Douglas was smelling the chance for extra reading time here. His mother's attention was elsewhere, and Douglas knew he could take advantage of that fact.

"Okay, Just a little while longer. Just till your hair dries." Joy knew exactly what her son was up to, but she let him get away with it this once.

" 'Night, Jack."

" 'Night, Douglas."

The boy started upstairs, but Joy called after him. "Wait! I want a kiss." She ran lightly after her son, and they kissed each other's cheeks with real affection.

" 'Night 'night. Sweet dreams."

" 'Night, Mom."

"I'm going to check the supper," Joy told Jack, and headed for the kitchen, where she opened the oven door. Steam came out, bringing with it savory aromas. Jack watched her from the kitchen doorway.

"What sort of things do you want me to say?" he asked, returning to the topic. Picking up a large spoon, Joy basted the roast and the vegetable cooking in a large enameled pan. Her voice was very level. "I want to stay friends with you, Jack. I need to know anything that would make that hard for you."

"I see," was all Lewis said in reply.

"We might as well know where we are."

Jack Lewis shied away from direct statements. The Oxford scholar in him demanded indirection, inference, even literary reference or allegory. But Joy Gresham was waiting for his answer. Jack knew he owed her an answer.

Above all, Jack didn't want to hurt Joy's feelings. He respected her and valued her too much as a companion. "You never can really tell what's going on, between people, can you?" he began. "People jump to conclusions. Sometimes it makes me quite

129

angry the way people aren't allowed to be . . . well, just friends."

"Like us, you mean." Joy's voice was very low, and she left the kitchen to continue setting the table.

"Like us," Jack said with a nod. "I don't mean to say that friendship is a small thing. As a matter of fact, I rate it as one of this life's most precious gifts."

"But—" She went on setting the table.

"But it shouldn't be turned into a watered-down version of something it is not."

"Such as—"

She wasn't going to give up easily, was she? She never had. "Such as, well, to give you one example, romantic love. Though that's not to say that friendship isn't, in its way—"

"A kind of love," finished Joy.

"A kind of love," agreed Jack, relieved. "I knew you'd understand."

"I understand better than that, Jack." She handed Lewis a bottle of burgundy and a corkscrew. "Will you open that for me, please?"

It was Jack's damn British reserve, a reticence where emotions were concerned, and a reluctance to discuss anything that might be unpleasant. Therein lay the greatest difference between them. Joy Gresham was never afraid to discuss anything with anybody at any time. Her frankness was as ingrained in her nature as Jack's reserve was in his.

"I understand that you are a bachelor and I am a divorced woman," she said with little emphasis, as though ticking items off a list. She folded two napkins into fan shapes. "Some people might suppose you to have romantic intentions towards me. You have no such intentions. You want to have this 'out in the open' because you care about me and don't want me to be hurt. Have I understood you correctly?" Joy stopped, waiting for a reply.

She was dead on the money. Joy Gresham seemed to understand him so well that Jack Lewis could almost believe she'd read his mind, only she'd read it out loud, which was more than he was ever prepared to do. He was amused, and yet a bit embarrassed.

"I don't know what to say," he said with a little laugh. Relationships were not a topic Jack felt comfortable in discussing; why couldn't they simply continue as they had been, just two friends who had important things—such as literature and belief—in common? Joy really had a sort of gift for dragging things out in the open, like the family cat bringing in a mouse.

"It's okay. I just said it. Wasn't so hard, was it?"

There was a muffled quality in Joy's voice that Jack had never heard before.

"I'm not used to this . . . whatever it is," Jack said stiffly. He wasn't sure whether or not to be offended. He wasn't even sure that what Joy said could be termed criticism. It was different from the scholarly banter he was used to with friends like Christopher Riley.

Joy shrugged. "Naming names. That's all." She went on calmly setting the table.

"Yes," he conceded.

"So now you don't have to be afraid of me, do you?"

"Good Lord! I was never afraid of you, Joy!" When she glanced at him, her eyebrow raised, he repeated it. "Why do you look at me like that? I was never afraid of you."

Did he really believe that? Was he so successful at deceiving himself? "I really am . . . very thankful . . . for everything you've done for me," Joy said sincerely.

"The least I can do. I'm sure there are far more substantial ways I can help, that you're not telling me about." Lewis felt far more confident on this ground, where he could remain detached and avuncular. A generous and openhanded man, he was happy when helping others in a material way.

It was pieces of himself that he was always stingy with.

"I don't want to exhaust your goodwill." She gave him a small smile, unlike her usual grins.

"No fear of that."

Turning away from him, Joy walked over to her desk and began fiddling with some papers so that she wouldn't have to look at Jack. Her words came slowly, and with effort and now she looked directly at him. "There is . . . something . . . which would really help me enormously. This really is very hard for me, Jack. If it's too much, you'd just say no, wouldn't you? No guilt, no evasion, no running away."

"Yes, I think I can just about manage that," smiled Lewis.

"Are you sure?" Joy turned around to face him. The expression in her eyes told him she was in dead earnest.

"Joy, I am capable of saying no."

When Joy Gresham finally told him, in a low tone and with hesitant words, what it was that would help her enormously, Jack listened carefully and with great surprise to every word. When she had finished, she looked at him expectantly, hope beginning to fade in her eyes. He took a long time to say anything but, when Jack Lewis spoke, he didn't say no.

S I X

Encaenia

He had to tell Warnie. When he returned to Oxford, Jack Lewis determined to let his brother know his plans as quickly as possible. Even so, he let two whole days go by before he said a word. Not that there was anything he had to hide, or anything to upset Warnie in the tidings, but Jack wasn't sure that Warnie wouldn't be upset anyway. Finally, he couldn't put it off any longer.

"There's something I ought to tell you, Warnie," he said as casually as he could. Lighting his pipe, he sucked on it thoughtfully.

"Mmm hmm?" Warnie looked up from the book in his lap.

The brothers were sitting in the garden at The Kilns, enjoying the afternoon spring sunshine, while their aged gardener Paxton pushed a noisy old lawnmower back and forth behind them. "I've agreed to marry Joy." Jack said quietly.

"You have?!" Warnie's eyes opened wide in surprise. He couldn't possibly think of anything more unexpected. Marriage! Jack?

"Yes. It seemed the right thing to do."

"It did?"

"Nothing to worry about, Warnie," said Jack, raising his voice in order to be heard over the mechanical chugging of the lawn mower. He smiled reassuringly at his brother.

"You see, what I have agreed to do is extend my British citizenship to her, so that she can go on living in England."

"By marrying her." Warnie was beginning to comprehend.

"Only technically."

"You're marrying Joy technically?" Now poor Warnie was even more confused than ever. And his sudden desire for a drink was quickly turning into desperation.

"Joy's visitor's visa has expired," Jack explained, "and the Home Office are not in all that much of a hurry to grant her a visa for permanent residence.

"A true marriage is a declaration before God, not before some government official," Jack said solemnly. "Joy will keep her own name. We will all go on living exactly as before. No one will know the marriage has taken place, apart from you, Somerset House, and the Home Office."

A dozen questions raced through Warnie's mind. How could they "all go on living exactly as before" if Jack was to be married to Joy Gresham? There were subleties here that were beyond Warnie Lewis. So far as he could understand, one was either married or not married, and that was all there was to it. But marriage as a technicality? Warnie had never heard such bally rot, but of course Warnie being Warnie he said nothing to Jack. Any questions lurking in Warnie's mind would have to continue unanswered.

The "technicality" took place soon after in a London registry office. It was a gray morning, threatening rain. Those present were the technical bride and the technical groom, the registrar, and one witness, Warnie. Joy was dressed in her best dress, a dark gray silk, and wearing a small spring hat with a little veil, and a precious pair of nylons she'd been saving for an occasion. Jack and Warnie were dressed in their second-best suits.

The registry office was dingy and institutional; it hadn't been painted in decades thanks to the war and the years of austerity following the war, but it made every effort to resemble a chapel, with curtains at the windows, vases of flowers standing about, and a large lectern, on which rested the registrar's book. The registrar himself was a slim and florid man in a neat dark suit, with rimless

glasses and a voice like butterscotch, resembling a
character out of a Dickens novel. He very much
enjoyed his role as marriage-maker and was determined to wring the maximum drama out of it.
"Take hands, please," he instructed.

Jack and Joy, standing before him, took hands,
Joy's right in Jack's left.

"Before you are joined in matrimony, I have to
remind you of the solemn and binding character of
the vows you are about to take."

No, thought Jack, *these vows are neither solemn
nor binding. It is done for the sake of expedience only,
and is not a marriage before God. This marriage is
purely and simply an act of kindness.*

"Mr. Lewis, if you will repeat after me, "I call
upon these persons here present—"

No, thought Jack, *these vows are neither solemn
nor binding. It is done for the sake of expedience only,
and is not a marriage before God. This marriage is
purely and simply an act of kindness.*

"Mr. Lewis, if you will repeat after me, 'I call
upon these persons here present—' "

"I call upon these persons here present—" Jack's
voice was strong and his tone matter-of-fact. He
didn't look at Joy.

"To witness that I, Clive Staples Lewis—"

"To witness that I, Clive Staples Lewis—"

"Do take thee, Helen Joy Gresham—"

"Do take thee, Helen Joy Gresham—"

"To be my lawful wedded wife."

"To be my lawful wedded wife."

"Mrs. Gresham, if you will repeat after me, 'I call upon these persons here present—' "

"I call upon these persons here present—" Joy's voice was low, and trembled a little. She didn't look at Jack.

"To witness that I, Helen Joy Gresham—"

"To witness that I, Helen Joy Gresham—"

"Do take thee, Clive Staples Lewis—"

"Do take thee, Clive Staples Lewis—"

"To be my lawful wedded husband."

"To be my lawful wedded husband."

"Do we have a ring?" asked the registrar.

"No," said Joy and Jack at the same time. There were to be no wedding bands, no public acknowledgement that these vows had ever been exchanged.

A few more sentences and the vows were completed. Helen Joy Gresham and Clive Staples Lewis were officially pronounced to be man and wife, and wrote their testatory signatures in the big registry book. The registrar beamed at them.

When the three of them came out of the registry office, it was raining. A very subdued Joy tugged her coat more tightly around herself and Jack put up his coat collar. Warnie unrolled his black umbrella and held it over Joy.

"That's that, then," Jack said.

"Can I buy you both a drink?" Joy asked.

Lewis frowned uncomfortably. "I'd love to, Joy, but I simply have to catch the twelve twenty-two. I have a lecture this afternoon. You know how it is."

"Of course, Jack," she nodded. "Off you go." Joy continued to smile as she watched his retreating back, until Jack Lewis rounded the corner and was out of sight. Then her smile disappeared instantly, and Joy suddenly looked pale and older than usual.

Warnie felt a pang of sympathy for her, his American technical sister-in-law. "I would be most grateful for that drink, Joy."

"That's kind of you, Warnie."

"I think I saw a pub down that road. Shall we risk it?"

"All right." She took his arm. "Go!" she said, and they set off together in the heavy downpour up the street under Warnie's large umbrella, in search of the pub.

"Well, that was quite an unusual experience," remarked Joy. In her voice a light sarcasm struggled with a touch of sadness, and lost.

"Yes. You must forgive Jack." Automatically, Warnie rose to a gallant defense of his brother, but privately he thought that Jack might easily have come with them for one drink. After all, this was supposed to be a festive occasion. Even if it wasn't—except in the technical sense, whatever that was—a real wedding, it did get Joy Gresham out of the immigration pickle she was in. Surely that benefit alone must be something worth celebrating.

"Oh, I'm getting to know him a little by now. I think I understand him. I'm very grateful to him." Joy made an effort to look happy, but her eyes were clouded.

"Nobody is to know, he tells me." Warnie cast a sidelong look at Joy.

"What he actually said was, 'It will be as if it never happened.'" Joy Gresham imitated Jack Lewis's pompous tones so exactly that Warnie laughed out loud as they turned into the pub doorway.

Mid-June arrived in a blaze of sunshine and very hot weather. Final exams, or "schools," as they're called, were in progress in the Examination Schools Building, where hopeful undergraduates scribbled feverishly in their booklets or stared at the ceilings for inspiration. For them, freedom was tantalizingly just around the corner. Soon they'd be Oxford graduates.

Sitting in their places in the Great Hall, under the magnificently carved oak screen, rich with medieval ornamentation, the dons were discussing their plans for the summer holidays. Now that the end of term was so near at hand, most would be traveling abroad.

"A great mistake, Jack. You'll live to regret it," Christopher Riley prophesied, helping himself liberally to the boiled potatoes.

"Regret what, Christopher?"

"Staying in this godforsaken place all summer. The day after Encaenia, I'm off."

"Where to, Christopher?" asked Rupert Parrish.

"Tuscany, where else?" Like so many Britons, Riley was carrying on an ongoing love affair with sunny Italy and her olive groves. Whom the gods love have a villa in Tuscany.

"We're going to the Loire," Rupert Parrish informed them as he chewed hard on a gristly bit of mutton. "Camping."

"Camping?!" Riley was aghast. Camping was something that undergraduate students did in order to make their few holiday pounds stretch as far as possible.

"I think I'll bring a guest this year," Jack said casually, buttering a bit of his roll.

"When Laura was alive, we once took the grandchildren camping," put in Harry Harrington nostalgically.

"Bring a guest, Jack?" Christopher Riley asked. "To what, pray?"

"Encaenia," answered Lewis.

Encaenia. One of the most beautiful annual ceremonies at Oxford, if not *the* most beautiful. Encaenia combines the glorious ritual of commencement exercises with the celebration of spring, with readings, and poetry, music and lectures. It includes a full-dress majestic university parade, filled with ancient symbolism representing centuries of British tradition. The ceremony, honoring graduate scholars, held in the 17th century Sheldonian Theatre, is always an eagerly sought invitation.

"Sleep outside the tent, Rupert, and smoke a cigar," Harrington advised.

"Whatever for?" demanded Rupert Parrish, mystified.

"Mosquitoes."

"Joy Gresham," said Lewis to Riley. "You've met her, remember?"

Indeed, Christopher *had* met her, had engaged her in hand-to-hand combat, and been roundly defeated by her. The wounds still smarted. "Not the American?" drawled Riley, as though he could barely recall her to mind. "Is she back in Oxford?"

"No, no," Jack said hastily. "She's in London. She wants to see the 'pageant of learning.' " He said this with quotation marks around the words, and with a deprecating shrug and a half smile.

Christopher saw right through the shrug. *Ah, so that way lies the land,* he thought with the slightest touch of contempt. Or was it envy? *C. S. Lewis has a Jewess.*

Down Broad Street, past hundreds of spectators with their cameras and their guidebooks, the Encaenia procession moved in stately grandeur. First came the beadles, dressed in black and carrying their silver wands of office; behind them the proctors marched by with their tasseled mortarboards on their heads. Following them came the scarlet-robed chancellor with his heavy gold neck chain bearing the large pectoral pendant showing the seal of Oxford and a Latin inscription. And, after the chancellor, the dons and the scholars of the colleges walked with measured tread, wearing their black and scarlet academic gowns. Among them was C. S. Lewis.

The procession approached the Sheldonian Theatre, which was not a theater at all but an assembly hall, built in 1663 by Christopher Wren. At that time, Wren was a professor of astronomy at Oxford, the Sheldonian Theatre was his first major architectural commission. But, with its impressive dome and cupola, this early work—named after the Archbishop of Canterbury Gilbert Sheldon, who commissioned the theater—is deemed one of the master architect's best. The composer Josef Haydn, receiving his honorary Doctor of Music degree from the university, conducted a performance of his "Oxford Symphony" at the Sheldonian. Like all of Oxford, the theater was rich in history.

Past the marble busts of the ancient Roman emperors which flank the entrance, the procession swept into the great hall of the Sheldonian to the strains of Handel played on a great-voiced organ. The chancellor assumed his seat on his elevated throne, while the other dignitaries took their places in seats below him to his right and left. Behind and above the chancellor, under the cupola, in the light of the many tall windows that ringed the dome, was a gallery where guests of the colleges could watch the pageantry below.

Joy Gresham, sitting with Warnie Lewis, regarded with fascination the pomp and the ritual beauty below. This kind of ceremonial show was so alien to Joy, not only as a democratic American, but to Joy as a left-wing despiser of displays of power, and yet she had to admit to herself that she was enjoying it, even when she had to stand when they played the national anthem. "God save the queen," sang the assembly loudly and lustily, while Joy, the former Communist, smiled in pleasure.

Nobody does ritual and tradition like the Brits, she thought.

It was a long and impressive ceremony, although tending to drag a little at times. During those times, Joy let her eyes wander around the magnificence of the Sheldonian, especially up to the great open dome of the ceiling, entirely painted in one vast allegory, with infant angels rolling back a huge canopy to reveal the blue heavens. It was as though they were sitting under those very heavens, and the angels were not made of plaster and paint, but flesh and blood. It was impossible not to be thrilled, even a bit overwhelmed, by the majesty of it all.

But no matter where Joy's eyes wandered, they always came back to Jack Lewis, seated below in his academic gown, surrounded by his fellow masters. The sight of him drew her like a magnet; he was not exactly conventionally handsome, but Jack was distinguished-looking, with a wide thoughtful brow, piercing blue eyes that could also become dreamy, and a noble sort of nose. Joy Gresham was proud to be C. S. Lewis's . . . guest. Every now and again, Jack would look up at the visitors' gallery, to find Joy smiling down at him. Whenever their eyes met, Jack found himself smiling, too.

Once or twice, when her eyes went wandering, they encountered another pair of eyes looking directly at her, black eyes, bright and sardonic, eyes that were viewing her with no great affection. Christopher Riley's eyes. He was watching her and his expression was tinged with contempt. The sight of him made Joy uncomfortable.

This year it was Magdalen College's turn to host the postgraduation tea party, and the party took place on the long stretch of lush green lawn between the Cloister building and the New Buildings, under the shade of the umbrella-sized leaves of a giant plane tree which was planted in 1801, according to the plaque in the ground nearby. Looking at the grass, Joy was reminded of the classic joke. An American asks a British gardener why English lawns are so fresh and verdant and thickly grown, and the Briton replies, "Plant the very best seed, water it well, and then roll it every single day for five hundred years."

Five hundred years. This lawn she was standing on was actually older than that, and the tree she was standing under was more than a century and a half old. As an American, Joy suddenly felt very raw and new, and had a flash of insight into the British character. No wonder they were so stolid and complacent and not in a hurry to change anything or to go anywhere; they had the slow march of the centuries in their blood.

All around Joy were the dons in their robes,

which contrasted sharply in the June sunlight with the flowery frocks, the broad-brimmed straw hats, and long white gloves of the university wives. Joy was standing with Warnie and Douglas, with Jack and a few of his university friends and their spouses. Not Christopher Riley, though. He was nowhere to be seen. But he had stationed himself where he could see Joy Gresham, and he watched with deep interest every little gesture and nod that passed between her and Jack. There was a mystery going on there, and secrets. Christopher Riley hated secrets unless they were his own.

"I feel distinctly underdressed," said Joy a little ruefully, eyeing the magnificence of Jack Lewis's black gown and scarlet hood.

"Just a sort of uniform, really," shrugged Jack, although he was secretly vain of his academic gown and well aware how much it became him.

"Jack's party frock," quipped Warnie.

That damned Riley is looking at me again, thought Joy. "Come here a moment, Jack." Joy beckoned him closer.

"What is it?"

"Something on your cheek." She raised her hand and brushed a tiny fleck off Jack Lewis's face. "There, it's gone now."

Catching sight of the gesture, Christopher Riley started in surprise. The intimacy of it, its familiarity absolutely flabbergasted him. Making certain to catch his eye, Joy tilted her head to one side and gave Riley her best sassy lift of the eyebrow, an expression that said very plainly, "What do you make of *thaat*, buddy?"

Not long after, Christopher cornered Warnie. "She's living in London now?" he demanded.

"Yes." No need to ask who.

"With her husband?"

"They're divorced."

Riley smiled ironically. "Why did I have a feeling you were going to say that?"

Sometime after, Jack, having paid polite respects to others at the party, caught up with Joy again. She seemed to him to be tired. "You all right?" he asked, concerned.

"Just a little exhausted," she admitted. "Would it be all right to sit down?"

"What? Yes, of course. You haven't seen my rooms yet. Let me show you." She was looking a trifle pale, he noticed suddenly.

They crossed to the New Buildings where Jack Lewis had his study, and climbed the flight of stairs, Joy much more slowly than usual. She had grown pale from fatigue and the pain she kept hidden. When they reached Jack's rooms, "Nescafé?" he offered.

"Sure."

Jack went to the room off his study, which served him as a little kitchen. There he kept an electric kettle, some tea, and sugar, and a small jar of Nescafé. He filled the kettle and clicked on the switch.

Joy walked over to the window and looked out, enjoying the sight of the party on the grass below, the tea-tent with its jaunty medieval look, the comfortable men and women strolling around the lawn or finding seats at the tables which had been set up. It was very festive, but a sudden stab of pain erased the smile on her face and made her stagger slightly. Limping to Lewis's desk, she sank gratefully into Lewis's old brown leather armchair and put her head back against the leather. "Oh, that's better; that's much better!"

Although she was talking more to herself than to him, Jack heard her and came out to see. "Perhaps you should change those shoes," he suggested.

Joy shook her head with vehemence. "I don't want to talk about it," she stated firmly. "I'm not going to stay long either. For all I know, I'm not even allowed to be here."

"Female guests are permitted between 10 A.M. and 8 P.M.," said Jack, taking her literally.

Joy checked her watch. "We're legal," she

149

grinned. "Jack, don't you sometimes just bust to share the joke?" she called into the little kitchen.

"What joke?"

"Here are your friends thinking we're unmarried and up to all sorts of wickedness, while all along we're married and up to nothing at all."

Lewis thought about it. He didn't find any of this a joke. Word had already seeped back to him through layers of scholarly Oxford dust that there were rumors going round about him and Mrs. Gresham. *Jack has a Jew*, said some snidely. Others were calling Joy Gresham "Lewis's Jewess" behind his back. Nobody dared to say this to his face, of course, but in a closed community like the university, there was always a spotlight on the doings of any of its members. "Which friends?"

"God, you can be hard work sometimes, Jack." Joy looked curiously around the study, at the large numbers of books, at the piles of papers, and the student workbooks on his desk. "So, what do you do here? Think great thoughts?"

"Teach, mainly."

"What do they do, sit at your feet and gaze up at you in awe?" The mental picture amused Joy, and she grinned.

"No, not at all."

"I bet they do."

"We have some fine old battles in here, I can tell you that," Jack said.

"Which you win."

Jack ducked back into the kitchen, hoping the kettle had come to a boil, even though he didn't hear it whistle. He wasn't sure he liked the direction this conversation appeared to be taking.

"It must be quite a boost for you, being older and wiser than all of them." Joy's eye fell on a copy of *The Lion, the Witch and the Wardrobe*, which Jack kept on his desk. "Not to mention your readers."

"What's that?" asked Jack, only half hearing.

"Your readers!" Joy looked at the small framed photograph on Jack's desk; it was of himself and his special group of friends at Oxford—Riley, Harrington, Parrish, and one or two others. It seemed to really irritate her. "And that gang of friends of yours. All very well trained not to play out of bounds. Then there's Warnie, of course," Joy continued. "No competition there."

"What are you talking about?" Jack seemed genuinely mystified.

By now there was no stopping Joy. Pain was exacerbating her irritation, yet, oddly, it seemed to make her think more clearly.

"And what about Christopher Riley?" Lewis could not begin to see what she was getting at. "He doesn't let me get away with anything. You know that."

"Except doubt, and fear, and pain. And terror." Joy's voice was vehemently raised.

"Where did all that come from?" Jack demanded.

"I've only just seen it," Joy said earnestly. "How you've arranged a life for yourself where no one can touch you." She stood up, and despite the searing pain in her leg, began to pace angrily around the study. "Where everyone close to you is younger than you, or weaker than you, or under your control."

What Joy was telling him as last was that she was sick of Jack Lewis always playing it safe. Life meant taking risks, putting your arse on the line and maybe getting it kicked, but so what? Playing it safe means you never change and you never grow, like a baby bird refusing to leave the nest and fly.

This was monstrously unfair, to be so provoked, and without reason! Jack felt a pang of indignation, mingled with anger at Joy, but he surpressed it. "Why are you getting at me, Joy? I thought we were friends."

She shook her head. There were circles of dark red in her pale cheeks, and her eyes glittered as with fever. "I don't know that we *are* friends. Not the way you have friends, anyway. Sorry, Jack."

Why has she suddenly turned on me this way? "I

don't understand." He stood rooted to the spot, completely dumbfounded.

"Yes, you do. You just don't like it. Nor do I." Without looking back, Joy headed for the door.

She was still angry when she left Jack's study, but she made her way down the stairs and went to find Douglas and Warnie. Jack didn't know whether to follow her or not, but the sudden whistling of the kettle distracted him. He remained behind, partly to regain control of himself. He was completely at a loss as to what had just happened here. Why was Joy angry with him? He'd never had angry words before with Joy Gresham. But he went to the window and watched her. He saw her rejoin her son and Warnie under the large plane tree. He saw her arm go affectionately around Douglas, saw her throw her head back in laughter at something Warnie had said. And puzzlement rose afresh in him.

The writing began to go badly. For the first time in his life, C. S. Lewis found that his work was affected by his personal feelings. He found it almost impossible to concentrate in his study at The Kilns; his house seemed to be haunted by Joy. He wrote, and he crossed out what he wrote; he groped for words, and his thoughts eluded him, ideas flashing through his mind, then darting out again as Joy Gresham's remembered face took their place. So he gathered up his notes and papers and moved his labors to Radcliffe Camera, the library he most favored in all of Oxford.

It was there that Lewis looked up from his desk one day to see Peter Whistler across the library, returning a large stack of books to the librarian. The sight of the student reminded Jack Lewis that it had been a long time since he'd seen Whistler. A prickling of conscience took Lewis back to the student's room that afternoon.

He found Whistler packing up his few belongings. The room was virtually bare of possessions.

"Are you off for the holidays?"

"No," Whistler said shortly. "I'm not coming back. I'm just going."

"Going? Going where?"

"London."

"Why? Is it money?" Something could be . . . should be . . . done for this student. Whistler's was an incisive mind that deserved encouragement.

"Not really." Peter Whistler wasn't giving an inch; whatever his reasons were for interrupting his education and turning his back on an Oxford degree, he was keeping them to himself.

"One more year, and you'd have your degree," protested Lewis, to whom this act was unthinkable.

"Then what? Teach, like you?" Whistler made the word "teach" sound like an expletive. He barely masked his contempt for Lewis and his precious status as a fellow and an Oxford don, even for Oxford itself.

Lewis felt defeated suddenly, assaulted on all sides. "I wonder what it is that everyone wants from me?" he said, not realizing that he was saying it aloud.

"That's the first question I've ever heard you ask that sounds like you don't know the answer," said Whistler. It was the same charge Joy had made, put into different words. That C. S. Lewis played it safe, and dealt only in matters he could handle easily, without trouble to himself.

"Is that good?" demanded Lewis. "Is that what you want? Ignorance? Confusion?"

"I don't think I see my way ahead quite as clearly as you do," Whistler said quietly.

He's being kind, thought Lewis with a flicker of surprise. *What he really means is that he doesn't want my help because it's the wrong kind of help, not what he needs but only what I choose to give. He's right.*

"Shadows," Jack said suddenly, half to himself.

"What?"

Jack Lewis shook his head and sighed. "One of my stories," he explained softly. "We live in the shadowlands. The sun's shining somewhere else.

Round a bend in the road. Over the brow of a hill . . .''

Lewis had not seen or spoken to Joy since Encaenia, at which time they hadn't parted as friends. Politely, yes, but not warmly, and with no plans to meet again in the immediate future. Lewis had journeyed to London since, but hadn't rung her or stopped in to see her. He'd thought of her often, but his images of Joy were obscured by doubts and confusion. Had she forgiven him? Did she want to hear from him? Again and again, when Jack Lewis's hand had reached out for the telephone, he always pulled it back.

But after his frustrating yet enlightening encounter with Peter Whistler, Lewis returned to The Kilns and dialed the number of Joy's London flat. He wanted to tell her that she wasn't alone in her perception of his character, that her opinion of him had been validated by another, and that he needed to talk, to apologize and sort things out between them.

Strange, but whenever Joy expressed her opinions about anything or anybody other than Jack Lewis, Jack always laughed, thinking how earthy and intelligent she was, how witty, how direct and clear-minded her judgments, how refreshing her bluntness. That same bluntness directed at him—

self brought only a reaction of close-minded resentment; he could see that now, quite plainly.

Also strange was this: Jack knew he possessed that quality of dispassion. He'd always considered it a good quality, a point in his favor. Now it appeared that others found it an unbearable characteristic, equating it with selfish indifference. Could there be something in that? Was Jack Lewis's vaunted detachment not an indication of a rational mind but a cold heart? He prayed it was not so.

At any rate, Jack resolved to get Joy on the telephone and tell her something of his revelations; he would ask to see her so that they could talk further. Surely she wouldn't refuse? Surely she was willing to be friends with him again?

Joy was sitting at her little desk, unhappily reviewing her dismal financial picture when the telephone rang. She was trying to decide which bills she could afford to pay this month, which creditors would wait until next month and which would not. The sound of the phone interrupted her in the middle of a column of addition, and she let it ring a few times. But soon she got up from her chair to answer it. She knew virtually nobody in London. Who else could it be ringing her but Jack? She hadn't spoken to him since Encaenia, not since she'd let him know some of

what was on her mind. Joy hadn't intended to hurt
Jack, but she knew he was hurt and angry; was it
possible that he'd forgiven her?

Joy hadn't told Jack everything. She'd kept from
him the simple secret that she had fallen in love
with him, and that she'd kept her love a secret,
afraid of what Jack might say, afraid of his turning
away from her in aversion. Slowly, little by little,
but inexorably, she had come to love this man to
whom she was "married" in name only, this man
whose center was untouched, and who kept himself uninvolved. His kindness to her as a friend
combined with his apparent indifference to her as
a woman was very painful for Joy to bear, and it
was out of this anguish that she had reproached
Jack Lewis for his detachment from life. Otherwise, why should it be of any concern to her that a
writer, theological thinker, and scholar like C. S.
Lewis should be a spectator of life rather than a
joyous participant in it?

The telephone was in another room, and Joy
began to hurry toward it. She very much wanted to
speak with Jack, to be good friends with him again.
He was the best friend she'd ever had, and Joy
missed him desperately. Suddenly, as she ran,
there was a hideous breaking sound, and a great
wave of agony rushed out to sweep over Joy, knock-
ing her to the floor and pinning her there, moaning

and weeping with pain. She couldn't move, she couldn't breathe. And there was nobody in the flat to help her. Nobody in the rest of the house could hear her, and Douglas would not be home from school for several hours.

The telephone rang and rang. At last it stopped, and there was silence in the room except for Joy's incessant moaning.

SEVEN

Like Blocks of Stone

Jack Lewis spent the entire night in the London hospital, much of the time pacing up and down the brightly lit corridor outside Joy's room. He needed to give vent to his nervous energy. The first thing he'd done was to install Joy Gresham in a private room, and the devil with the expense or the free wards of the National Health! He also passed many long hours at Joy's bedside, watching her sleep deeply under the heavy injections of morphine. He thought he had never seen anyone so frail and vulnerable; all her vitality had disappeared, and she was so small and thin that he was afraid she would vanish away the next time he blinked. Joy's face was as white as the bleached hospital bed linen, and only her tumbled hair made a scattering of color on the pillow.

Jack would sit looking at Joy for as long as he could stand it, then out into the corridor once more, to pace its length back and forth like a caged leopard. He felt so damned paralyzed! His power-lessness in the face of this emergency was galling to him. He wanted desperately to take Joy's pain to himself, to free her of it and carry it for her, but he realized it was impossible. Even prayer couldn't accomplish that. The hardest thing was not know-ing whether Joy was going to live or die. No . . . that wasn't true. The hardest thing was the thought of losing her, when he'd only just found her.

When he'd first arrived from Oxford, forceful and demanding, Joy's doctors were reluctant to tell Lewis anything. They kept their diagnoses avail-able only for the next of kin. But Jack stood his ground and insisted, at the last ditch revealing that Joy was in fact his legal wife. Only then did Dr. Craig part with the diagnosis: inoperable cancer.

Cancer! That illness of all illnesses the most dreaded, the most painful, the deadliest. How was it possible? How could God let this happen? Joy was so good, so loving, so honest, where was the logic, the divine purpose in striking her down? And so the eminent popular theologian C. S. Lewis, the distant man who was so reassuring in the face of others' pain, was finally caught in his own trap, asking the same questions of God that others asked of him, only now he was so much less certain of the answer. He prayed hard, he listened for God to speak, but heard only silence.

Meanwhile, there were practical matters to be dealt with. Warnie, bless him, had rallied immediately and taken care of everything; he was tireless. When the summoning phone call came from the hospital, Warnie had asked no questions of Jack. He just grabbed up his old mac off the peg, jammed on his hat, and hurried along with Jack to the London train. Once in London, Warnie had gone directly to Joy's flat, to bundle Douglas up and carry him off to The Kilns, where he'd be well looked after. Then, back again on the next train down to London, without even stopping for a cup of tea or a whiskey. Now he was coming down the hospital corridor, looking for his brother. From the depth of his anguish, Jack rallied just a little at the sight of that beloved old face, so honest and trustworthy.

"How is she?" Warnie asked quietly. Jack Lewis shrugged silently and shook his head. "I'm so sorry, Jack."

"I just want her to be well again, you see," said Jack, as simply as a child.

"Of course you do. We all do." Warnie had long ago come to care about Joy Gresham, and he recognized—before Jack did—that Joy loved Jack very much.

"What a dangerous world we live in, Warnie." A deep sigh, almost a groan, tore from Lewis's bosom.

Warnie put one reassuring hand on Jack's shoulder. "Why don't you get some sleep? You've been up all night, Jack." He spoke with sympathy, although he knew that his brother wouldn't give up his post outside Joy's room.

Jack shook his head. "I can't sleep. I've never felt more awake in my life." Jack's arms and hands moved restlessly; his shoulders twitched under his jacket and his feet made circular patterns on the hospital linoleum. "You see, Warnie, we just haven't had time. It's all too soon."

"Too soon for what?"

"I haven't had time, you see, Warnie." Jack had such a look of anguish on his face that Warnie suffered just seeing him.

"Time for what, Jack?"

"Time to . . . Oh, I don't know . . . talk . . . say things. . . ."

Now Warnie understood what his brother was trying to tell him. Jack loved Joy. At last, after years of evasion and denial, he had fallen in love and was finally acknowledging it. It took an explosion of a life-threatening illness to make Jack finally face himself and the truth he'd been suppressing. Now he was terrified of losing her.

When exactly Jack had fallen in love with Joy,

Jack didn't know. Had he loved her for a long time, refusing to admit it even to himself? He didn't know that, either. But now he was agonizing over what he considered to be time wasted, time he could have spent in openly loving Joy and being with her. Warnie felt a rush of affection and sympathy for his younger brother. "It doesn't take long," he said quietly.

"No, I suppose not."

"Whatever it is, I should just say it."

Jack looked gratefully at his brother. Once again, Warnie's honest simplicity was the map pointing to the right direction.

"Yes, you must be right, Warnie. But it's difficult, you see."

"Yes. I do see that."

"I just want her to be well again. That's all."

Dr. Craig emerged from Joy's room. "Dr. Craig, this is my brother Warnie."

The two men nodded. "Mr. Lewis, your wife—"

"How is she? Any change?" A brief flash of hope lit Lewis's face.

The doctor shook his head. "We've made her as comfortable as we can. Otherwise, there's nothing further to report."

"How much has she been told?"

Dr. Craig scowled. "She's been told the cancer has eaten away her left femur."

"Oh, no," Jack said softly, almost a groan.

"She knows it's serious," the doctor continued. "How can she not know? Her thigh bone snapped like a frozen twig."

Jack Lewis winced at the physician's words; it was more bitter than gall to imagine Joy in such pain of body and mind. And to think that she had lain there, on the floor, weeping in agony, her bone broken, until Douglas had returned from school to find her there! What torture it must have been for them both!

"Can anything be done?" Warnie Lewis asked the doctor quietly.

Jack wheeled on his brother. "She's dying, Warnie."

"That's putting it more starkly than I would choose," the doctor protested.

Jack whirled to confront him. "No, but it's true, isn't it?"

"The cancer is very advanced," Dr. Craig conceded.

With Joy still sleeping soundly under the narcotic, Jack allowed himself to be taken by Warnie to a nearby café, where they sat dismal and silent over cold bacon sandwiches and mediocre coffee. All his life, Jack Lewis had been grateful for the quiet, soothing presence of his brother, and never more so than in this crisis. Just to be with Warnie was calming, and it was a blessing, too, not to have to speak. Jack didn't think he could say a word without weeping, but Warnie understood his anguish without being told. At last, they parted, Warnie to return to Oxford and Douglas, Jack to his bedside vigil.

The dam he'd built to contain his feelings, built so laboriously over so many years, burst at last, and the long-contained waters of emotion rushed out to flood his soul. Jack Lewis surrendered himself to loving Joy Gresham as he had once surrendered himself to loving Jesus Christ, and once again, he prayed that his love might redeem him.

It was only toward evening that Joy finally opened her eyes. "Hallo, Joy," he said softly.

"Jack?" Her voice was so weak it was barely a whisper.

"Don't talk if it hurts."

Joy licked her cracked lips. "Where's Douglas?"

"He's staying with us for the moment. I'll bring him to see you as soon as you're up to it."

"Thank you," she said with relief. Her eyelids fluttered closed, as though she could barely keep them open. Then, with a great effort, Joy dragged her lids up again. "Is there any water?"

Jack stood up stiffly, poured a half glass of water from the hospital carafe, and held it to Joy's lips.

"Did you visit me before?" Joy asked weakly.

"Yes. A couple of times."

"I thought so." The morphine was wearing off, leaving Joy less groggy, but the pain, like the monster in a fairy tale, was lying in wait for her, its curved claws and sharp teeth stained red with blood.

"They're going to operate on the broken bone tomorrow," Jack said quietly.

Joy tried to smile. "Sorry, Jack. I didn't mean to cause you all this bother."

"Don't talk nonsense. You're the one who's having the bother," he told her crisply, while his heart wept at the sight of her suffering.

Joy licked at her lips again; they were very dry. "What I mean is, I don't expect you to take care of me."

"Oh? And who do you expect to take care of you?"

"You know what I'm trying to say," Joy whispered with an enormous effort. The pain monster had renewed its gnawing at her weakened body.

Jack opened his mouth to tell Joy he loved her, but he realized that this was not the time. She was far too weak. "Who else should be looking after you but me? You are my wife," was all he said.

"Technically." Joy's attempt at a smile was little more than a crease at the corners of her lips, but her spirit was real; it shone through the pain.

"Then I shall look after you technically."

Joy struggled to raise her head from the pillow, but it was a hopeless task. "Jack, I have to know how bad it is. They won't tell me."

"That's because they're not sure themselves." The lie choked his throat, and he found it difficult to look at her while her dark eyes were begging him.

"Please, Jack."

"I don't know any more than they do, Joy."

"Before Douglas gets here. I need to know."

The pull of Joy's honesty forced Lewis to accede to her need. She was right; the boy would have to know and Joy alone would have to deal with her son. The words were torn from his inner soul, and they were the most brutal words anyone had ever spoken. "They expect you to die."

Shutting her eyes, Joy nodded. "Thank you." Then a pale ghost of her mocking smile tugged at her lips. "What do you say, Jack? I'm a Jew. I'm divorced. I'm broke. And I'm dying of cancer. Do you think I get a discount?"

Her attempt at humor, the shadow of the old Joy, broke Jack Lewis's heart. "Oh, Joy," he said with a gut-wrenching sigh, and he felt the sting of tears behind his eyelids. His eyes met Joy's and he tried to smile.

"You know something?" whispered Joy. "You seem different. You look at me properly now."

For a moment, he didn't understand her meaning. "Didn't I before?" he asked.

"Not properly."

Then he understood. It was true; for as long as he'd known her, Lewis had avoided the clarity and directness of Joy's soul, run away from confrontation with the deepest essence of her. She was a "friend," Jack had told himself, someone to match wits with, someone to be comfortable with, a companion for cups of tea and glasses of wine and intellectual discussions of poetry and literature, but nobody to look at "properly." That would be too dangerous; it might lead to involvement and inconvenience, to the breaking down of the cloistered little scholarly life he'd built up for himself so carefully and over so many years. Oh, what a fool he'd been!

"I don't want to lose you, Joy." Jack wrenched the words from the misery in his heart; there was no way they could express the despair that threatened to overwhelm him.

"I don't want to be lost." A spasm of agony overtook her and Joy's entire body trembled in pain. A low moan escaped her, ending in a thin scream.

"Nurse!" shouted Jack frantically, but nobody came. "Nurse!" he cried again, and ran out into the corridor to find help for Joy. At last a young sister came on the run, pushing past the distraught Lewis into the room, and bent over the bed, examining Joy.

"Is this pain really necessary?" demanded Jack, torn between agony and anger. Joy moaned and writhed on her bed, attempting to escape the monster of pain that was flaying her alive.

"I'll fetch the doctor." The nurse hurried out. In a moment or two, Dr. Craig came in, with the nursing sister behind him. Seeing Joy Gresham's suffering, he filled the hypodermic with morphine and injected it quickly into a vein. Within seconds, Joy's tortured face relaxed, and she fell back into a drugged sleep.

So that was the way it was to be. Either Joy would be awake and in unbearable pain, or she would be lying unconscious, drugged. Either way, it would not be Joy herself lying on that bed, but something the cancer had created. It was unthinkable. His eyes brimming with tears, Jack Lewis sat down on the chair beside her bed, to keep vigil again for his heart's dearest. He tried once more to pray, but all he could think of was *Why, God? Why?*

Warnie watched Douglas climb in between the sheets, and tucked the bedclothes around him.

"There we are," he said, handing the boy the folded paper boat they had made together. "We'll make another one tomorrow. Now what? Lights out?"

"No. I read in bed," answered the boy.

"Got your book?" Nodding, Douglas pulled a well-worn book out from underneath his pillow. "How long are you allowed to read?"

"One chapter," Douglas said truthfully.

"One chapter, then," Warnie agreed.

"I want to be awake when Jack gets back," Douglas said anxiously.

"That shouldn't be long now."

"He'll say good night, won't he?"

"Of course."

But when Jack Lewis arrived at The Kilns late that evening, weary to the bone from his long days in London, Douglas was already asleep. Jack walked slowly into the study, where Warnie was sitting with his pipe and a book. Warnie looked up expectantly, his craggy face a question mark, but Jack shook his head without a word. The news was not good. The news was as bad as it could be.

"I promised Douglas you'd say good night," Warnie said quietly.

Jack nodded and went slowly up the stairs. He moved like a very old man, with stiffness in all his limbs. His head ached atrociously. He was worn out completely by lack of sleep, by the tension in his muscles, and, most of all, by the love and the fear which ripped away at his soul.

The lights were still on in Douglas's room, but the boy was sleeping soundly, his book lying open on the bed covers. For a few moments, Jack Lewis stood watching Douglas sleep. With his eyes closed, the boy's resemblance to his mother— "From here down I look like Mom"—was even more striking. Lewis sighed deeply; he picked up the book and put it away, and leaned down to pull the covers up over Douglas's shoulders. He hesitated for a second, then he acted from the heart, kissing Douglas on his boyish forehead. He had never kissed a child before, but this was Douglas, Joy's son, and almost his own. This was yet another person with a strong claim on him. Straightening up, Lewis turned the light out quietly and left the room.

Back in Oxford, Jack Lewis and this woman Joy Gresham were the chief topic of conversation at Magdalen College. Lewis kept rushing back and forth, between the hospital in London and his responsibilities in Oxford, and it was taking its toll on him. Once the initial surprise had passed, and his fellow dons accepted the fact that Jack was indeed involved in some way with Joy Gresham, and that she was dying of cancer and not expected to live out the month, there was an enormous uprush of sympathy for both of them, especially for Jack, who was a valued member of their closed circle. The wicked little mockeries and nasty jibes were a thing of the past, and no more did one hear the malicious phrase "Lewis's Jewess." Heaven alone knows what the gossip would have been had Oxford found out the two were—if only technically—married.

The college chaplain emerged from the chapel, where he'd left Jack on his knees, praying to his maker, beseeching strength and understanding. It was plain that Jack wished to pray alone, without Harry's professional intercession. Even though he was a churchman, it was hard for the Reverend Harrington to know what to say to him, Jack's pain in the face of the calamity of a dying friend was obviously so great. Harry shook his head, hoping that his dear old friend would not be crushed under the burden he was carrying. Christopher Riley was passing by just then, on his way to a lecture, and he hailed the chaplain.

"Have you seen Jack? How is he?"

Harry gestured toward the chapel. "It's knocked him completely off balance," said Harry Harrington mournfully.

"Sad business," Christopher Riley agreed.

"Has he said anything to you?"

"About her?" asked Riley. Harrington nodded. No need to identify "her." "No. Nothing."

Inside the fine Gothic chapel, daylight streamed in through the magnificent stained glass windows, fragmenting into jeweled rainbows and spreading their radiant colors over the stone floor, the majestic altar, and the heavily carved pews. It was a sight of inspiring beauty, but Jack Lewis was unconscious of the beauty. He knelt in his pew, his head bowed over his clasped hands, and he prayed to God. His prayers were silent and even incoherent, very unlike his former articulate prayers. In these prayers there was a kind of desperation, and the word "love" was spoken over and over without words. His mind and soul in torment, Jack prayed for a quarter of an hour, then he stood up a little stiffly, and made his way to the door.

Riley and Harrington were still standing outside the chapel, their sad thoughts on their friend Jack, when Jack emerged from the chapel. Seen this way suddenly, without his having time to compose himself, Jack Lewis appeared to his friends to be a changed man.

Jack's face, usually ruddy with health, was pale and drawn, and his bright blue eyes were shadowed. Although he was clean-shaven, he'd obviously been distracted during the shave, because here and there small patches of growth had escaped the razor undetected. His hair, usually worn combed back and tight to the skull, was unkempt. But it was the expression on his face that would melt a stone. It was the expression of a man unable to comprehend the forces which gripped and buffeted him; Jack Lewis looked helpless. Nobody but Warnie had ever seen Lewis helpless before, not being in control of events was not in his working vocabulary. At least not since he was nine years old and his mother had gone away through the door of death.

"Oh, Christopher." Jack's voice seemed to come from very far away.

"I'm so sorry about all this, Jack," said Riley, and he meant it. It hurt him to see his old friend's confidence so shaken and Jack himself in so much misery.

"Yes. Yes, Christopher, thank you." It was obvious his thoughts were elsewhere. Riley squeezed Jack's arm in silent reply, and continued on his way to his students.

Lewis fell into step beside Harry Harrington. "It's all come too soon, you see. Her affairs aren't in order. What's to happen to Douglas, for example?"

"I suppose his father—" suggested the chaplain.

175

Jack shook his head firmly. "She doesn't want that. He drinks, you know. He's an alcoholic."

"There must be other relatives, Jack. I mean, it's not as if . . ." Harrington's words trailed off.

"Not as if what?"

"Well, she's your friend, of course, but she's not . . . well . . . family." Harrington's cheeks felt hot; this was a most uncomfortable conversation.

"Not my wife?" demanded Jack.

Harry uttered a nervous laugh. "No, of course not."

"Of course not," said Jack bitterly. "Impossible. Unthinkable." An American, his flat words implied. A Jew. A divorced woman. Totally unsuitable.

"I only meant—"

Jack turned his face to Harry, and tears glistened in his eyes. "How could Joy be my wife? I'd have to love her, wouldn't I? I'd have to care more for her than for anyone else in this world. I'd have to be suffering the torments of the damned at the prospect of losing her." The words burst out of Jack Lewis; he was powerless to control them.

Tears! Harrington had never seen his friend in tears. So that was it! They were married! And he loved her! In all the speculation going around Oxford, in all the gossip, this was the possibility that had never been thought of. Astonished by

Jack's revelation, Harry Harrington drew in his breath. "I'm sorry, Jack. I didn't know."

Lewis sighed deeply. "Nor did I, Harry. Nor did I."

A few days later, after Joy's operation, Warnie brought Douglas in from Oxford to visit his mother. Exhausted by the pain and her recent surgery, Joy was very weak, and could do little more than lie in bed, propped up on several pillows, and stroke her son's hand. Douglas sat by his mother's bedside, trying very hard not to cry. Even so, they were very happy to see each other again.

Warnie and Jack stood in the background, just watching. The thoughts of both men went traveling back many years, to another time in another hospital, to another mother on her deathbed, to other small sons who tried manfully to keep their tears from showing.

"Remember?" whispered Jack to Warnie.

"Oh, yes."

"Better take him home," Jack whispered. "I'll stay a little longer, catch the eight-forty." Nodding, Warnie stepped forward and put his hand on Douglas's shoulder.

"Ever had toasted tea cakes, Douglas? The secret's in the butter, oozing down your fingers. Shall we go and find some?" The boy nodded, and stood up at once. With her eloquent eyes, Joy silently thanked Warnie, who smiled back at her with fondness.

"Lots of butter," he told the boy as they left the hospital room. "Oozing with butter. That's the secret."

As soon as they'd left, Jack slipped into the chair beside the bed and sat watching Joy. Under heavy medication and wiped out by the emotional effort of seeing Douglas, she kept drifting in and out of consciousness. At last she opened her dark eyes and looked at Lewis.

"Are you staying?" she whispered.

"Yes for a while." The expression in her eyes told him, I'm glad.

Her smile, wan yet warm, went directly to his heart. He'd given a great deal of thought to what he was about to say, and now he set the matter before Joy. "I want to marry you, Joy," he declared. "I want to marry you before God and the world."

Joy smiled more broadly, although still weakly. "Make an honest woman of me," she whispered.

Tears stung Lewis's eyes as he shook his head vehemently. "No, not you, Joy. It's me who hasn't been honest. Look what it takes to make me see sense."

"You think I've overdone it?" A flash of the old mocking Joy stabbed Jack in his heart.

"Please don't leave me, Joy," he begged.

Her eyes shut again. When they opened, she spoke very slowly. "Jack, about this . . . marrying. Back home, where I come from . . . we have . . . a quaint . . . old custom. When the . . . guy's . . . made up his . . . mind he wants . . . to marry the girl . . . he asks her. It's . . . called . . . pro . . . posing."

"It's the same here," smiled Jack.

"Did I . . . miss it?"

Lewis took her bone-thin hand up from the bed and held it in his while he looked deeply into her beloved face. Then this confirmed bachelor in his mid-fifties, overwhelmed by love for the first time in his existence, proposed marriage, speaking words that he'd never expected to say in his lifetime. "Will you marry this foolish, frightened old man, who needs you more than he can bear to say, and loves you even though he hardly knows how?"

With the smallest, almost imperceptible movement, Joy Gresham nodded her head. "Just this once." Then her eyelids closed.

Up to now, Jack had been able to spare very little time for Douglas, but that would have to change. Marrying Joy would change everything. But first, Jack would have to talk with Douglas about the impending marriage. Joy had told her son their news on his last visit to the hospital, but it was up to Jack to . . . ask for the boy's blessing, he supposed. It was no small matter. On this clear, warm afternoon, Lewis went looking for the boy and found him in one of Douglas's favorite haunts, lying on his stomach on the pier over the small lake, sailing a little paper boat, like the poet Shelley. "We don't seem to have had much time to talk," Jack began.

"I'm okay." Douglas didn't look up, but went on poking with his stick at the fragile little craft.

"Your mother and I—"

"Why did we ever have to come to this stupid country—?" the boy burst out suddenly.

"Douglas—" said Jack helplessly.

"We were all right where we were. I told Mom, but she wouldn't listen." His words and expression was resentful, but Lewis understood that the resentment arose out of pain, not anger.

"Does my dad know she's sick? Did anybody tell him?"

"Yes, he's been told."

The paper boat sailed out of reach, into a clump of marshy reeds, and remained there, held fast by the thick cattails. It began to disappear slowly under the surface of the pond. "It's sinking now," Douglas said. "I don't care." But Jack knew he did care; Jack understood that to Douglas the boat was in some way a symbol of Joy herself, frail and vulnerable, and now out of reach and sinking, unretrievable. Douglas's eyes were filled with tears.

Jack decided to try again. "I know your mother's talked to you . . . about . . ." he started again, tentatively.

"Yup."

"Would that be all right with you?"

"Yup."

"It would make me happy. And I think it would make her happy, too."

"Okay." And with that one word, "okay," Joy's word, the blessing was given. A great weight lifted off Jack Lewis's spirit. *That*, at least, was all right. He had Douglas's blessing.

On the day of her wedding to Jack Lewis, Joy Gresham refused any injections of painkiller. "I want to be awake for this," she told her nurse. "I don't want to miss a minute."

While the nursing sister combed Joy's hair, Joy held up a hand mirror, and examined herself anxiously. Did she look pretty? A little more lipstick maybe? A touch of rouge? If only she weren't so pale, with those big dark rings around her eyes. And her face had grown so thin, the cheekbones stood out in sharp ridges! But when her thoughts turned inevitably to Jack, Joy smiled into the mirror. She had loved him for such a long time, and now he loved her back. Now they would truly be man and wife, as Jack said, before God and the entire world. Was it dumb to be so happy when you were dying of cancer?

For this second wedding ceremony, Jack brought flowers, a cheerful bouquet of pretty blooms for Joy's bedside table. There were wedding guests, too. Warnie and Douglas, of course, and the nurse and Dr. Craig. Propped up on pillows, Joy smiled happily as Jack took her small hand and held it in both of his. The Anglican priest who performed the marriage was a young man, Father John Fisher, the chaplain of the hospital. Jack's voice, as he spoke the traditional Christian vows, resonated with love and happiness. Joy's voice was also clear, although it was not strong.

"I, Joy, take thee, Jack."

"To have and to hold, from this day forward—" said Father Fisher.

"To have and to hold, from this day forward—"

"For better, for worse—"

"For better, for worse—"

"For richer, for poorer—"

"For richer, for poorer—"

"In sickness and in health—"

"In sickness and in health—"

"To love, cherish, and obey—"

"To love, cherish, and obey—"

"Till death us do part."

"Till death us do part."

"The ring?"

This time there was a ring, a wide, plain golden band. Warnie stepped forward and handed it to the priest, who placed it in his Bible and gave it to Jack. Jack slipped it over Joy's thin ring finger, while the priest bound both their hands together with his vestment and made the sign of the cross over them.

"With this ring I thee wed—"

"With this ring I thee wed—" Jack's eyes never left Joy's face as he repeated the priest's words and completed his vows.

"With my body I thee worship—"

"With my body I thee worship—"

"With all my worldly goods I thee endow."

"With all my worldly goods I thee endow."

"Those whom God hath joined together, let no man put asunder."

Thank God, thought Jack, as he bowed his head over Joy's hands. The ring shone brightly on her left hand. Thank God we were allowed to do this before it was too late. And thank God for bringing Joy to me, even now. For no matter what happens, she is my chief happiness.

For the first time, Jack and Joy kissed, their lips joining with deepest love.

In work and in prayer, Lewis found the only real distractions from his misery. So he prayed, and he taught, and he wrote, and he lectured. He continued to accept speaking engagements, especially in London, so that he could be at Joy's hospital before and afterward.

In his most popular lecture, on the divine purpose of suffering, Lewis made an important change. No longer did he need to use anecdotes about strangers, letters from readers, or examples from newspaper clippings. Now he had the perfect example drawn from his own life. Now Lewis's hands did not rest easily on his lectern, but gripped the lectern tightly, so that his knuckles showed white.

Lewis looked out over his audience, but he didn't see any of their faces. The only face he could visualize was small, and very white, and twisted in pain. The eyes were closed.

"Recently, a friend of mine, a brave and good woman, collapsed in terrible pain. One minute she seemed fit and well. The next minute she was in agony. She is now in hospital, suffering from cancer. Why? If you love someone, you don't want them to suffer. You can't bear it. You want to take their suffering onto yourself. If even I feel like that, why doesn't God?" At long last, this was no longer Lewis's answer, but his question.

❧

E I G H T

Coming Home

The Oxford station of British Railways and the platform for the London train had become by now almost a second home to Lewis. Just about every day, but never less frequently than five days a week, he stood waiting for the cars that would carry him to his wife's hospital bed. As soon as his classes were over, the same taxi would pick him up outside Magdalen College and carry him to the station.

The ride was not a long one in any case, an hour and three-quarters, but to Lewis it seemed no time at all, so deep was he always sunk in his own thoughts. He couldn't concentrate on his newspaper, and would soon lay it aside unread. He took very little notice of the station stops or of the English countryside speeding past the carriage window. He took no notice whatever of other passengers, so he was taken by surprise this day to hear his name spoken out loud in a familiar voice.

"Mr. Lewis?"

Jack looked up. A young man, no more than twenty-six or -seven, had just entered the carriage searching for an empty seat. His thoughts being so far away, at first Jack didn't recognize him. Then the face intruded into his consciousness, and he could put a name to it.

"Peter Whistler," he said. The boy was more neatly dressed than Lewis had ever seen him, and his hair was tidily combed. Otherwise, it was the same Whistler, the same restless spirit showing in his face.

"Yes, it's me."

Lewis was surprised to hear himself offering to buy Whistler a beer, and even more surprised when his former student accepted at once. They made their way gingerly down the swaying train corridor to the buffet car and ordered a couple of pints.

The beer was unspeakable, warm and barely drinkable.

"It's warm," complained Lewis.

"That's all right," joked Whistler. "The Brit Rail coffee is always cold." Lewis laughed, and they both laughed together. Standing companionably side by side, they sipped at their flat beers and stared out the train window.

"Funny how things work out," Lewis said at last.

"I've not noticed that they do," Peter Whistler replied.

"No. You're probably right."

" 'Fight me. I can take it,' " quoted Whistler. Lewis smiled, surprised and pleased that the young man could recall something of his class, even if it was only that. But he was hardly in the mood for a verbal scrap. Standing by helpless day after day and watching his wife suffer the torments of the damned had drained a lot of the fight out of Lewis. It was peace, not conflict, that was his ambition now.

"So what are you doing these days?" he asked his former student.

Whistler took a pull at his drink. "Teaching. Feel free to give a hollow laugh."

"No." Jack Lewis shook his head. "I suspect you're a born teacher."

"I do turn out to be quite good at it," conceded Whistler grudgingly, but Lewis could detect a note of pride in the young man's voice.

"Didn't you tell me your father is a teacher?"

"Yes." For a second he hesitated, then Peter Whistler added, "He died. A few months ago."

"I'm sorry," said Lewis sincerely.

188

Whistler nodded, and bit at his lip, forcing the tears back. "I miss him. I loved him very much."

"Did he know that?" Lewis looked earnestly at the boy.

Whistler thought the question over. "I think so. I think he knew."

"One has to say things," Lewis continued. "The moment passes, and you're alone again."

"Yes."

" 'We read to know we're not alone.' That's what he said, wasn't it? I've not forgotten that."

Whistler nodded, overcome by emotion and unable to speak. Once more, it struck Jack Lewis how inevitable it was, how God-ordained, that every human being should suffer loss. Without exception, every single person in the world would know at some time the excruciating pain of loss. For some—like young Whistler—it would come from losing a loved one; for others, it would be having nobody to love. And Jack suspected that far and away the first might be easier to bear. Because, with all the agony that he and Joy were going through, separately and together, in loving her and in knowing that she loved him Lewis was happier than he'd ever been in his life. Wasn't that some absurd divine paradox? Did it mean that God had a sense of humor?

* * *

It was Dr. Craig's recommendation that once Joy's condition had stabilized somewhat she should begin receiving radiation treatments. Radiation was something fairly new and quite radical, to bombard the ailing human body with radioactive isotopes, but in some cases it had proven effective in preventing the spread of cancer. Radiation was not without its drawbacks; it was not entirely safe. At best the patient suffered burns, and the treatment was grueling and debilitating. But it was the only possible option that offered the smallest shred of hope. After discussing it at length with both Joy and the physician, Lewis agreed to radiation therapy for Joy, and signed papers to release the hospital from responsibility in case the treatment should prove injurious rather than beneficial.

So, while Jack Lewis prayed in the hospital chapel, attendants wheeled Joy Lewis through a door marked DANGER: RADIATION HAZARD and into a small room like a cell, and left her lying there with the X ray machine, while the deadly rays from the machine invaded her body and attacked her cells. They did this twice, three times, then many times. It was all part of the suffering that Joy was forced to endure in the hope of becoming better. Or at least in the hope of not dying right away.

After weeks of prayer, and weeks of Joy's intense

pain, and the conviction that his wife would die at any moment, Jack Lewis began to believe that he was perceiving a change in Joy. For some days now, Jack had been harboring the suspicion that Joy might be possibly getting better. The signs were miniscule at first and hard to detect, but to his careful eye, so focused on Joy, it seemed to Jack that she had a little more energy than previously, a touch of color in her cheeks, and that she was beginning to spend fewer hours in her opiate-drugged sleep. Today, when he looked in on her, Joy was positively vivacious. Anybody could recognize the early signs of . . . what? . . . a recovery? Did he dare to hope?

"I'll be back very soon, darling." And, kissing his wife's brow, Jack went looking for Joy's doctor.

Of course, Dr. Craig was as elusive as a weasel. Inviting Lewis into his office, he showed him two sets of X rays of Mrs. Gresham's thigh and pelvis, hanging over a lighted box on the wall. The first set was taken when Joy had first entered the hospital; the second set were taken only the day before. The films were a total mystery; Lewis could only stare at them without being able to interpret them. On tenterhooks, Lewis waited for the physician's explanation of the X rays.

"Well," began Dr. Craig, "I think I'm in no danger of overstating the case if I say no news is good news. Given the seriousness of her condition, we have reason to be cautiously optimistic."

Cautiously optimistic? Medical jargon? What the hell did that mean? Jack pressed for a real answer. "I'm sorry, Doctor, but I don't understand a word you're saying. It would help me if you would use terms I'm familiar with, like 'getting better,' 'getting worse.' 'Dying.' "

The doctor shrugged. "I'm afraid none of those words meet the case. What seems to be happening is that the rate of spread of the disease is slowing down."

"You mean she's getting better?"

"She's not worse." Again that insufferable non-committal elusiveness, the trademark of the medical profession.

This was maddening. "Is not-being-worse better than being-worse?" persisted Lewis.

"Put it like that, yes." But the commitment was a grudging one; Dr. Craig was a man who, if he made a mistake, would always err on the side of caution.

"Did you expect her to make it this far?" It was a direct question, allowing only a yes or no answer, and it cornered Dr. Craig at last.

"Frankly, no," he admitted.

"Right," said Lewis, and headed back to Joy's room. Today the hospital room seemed a lot less cheerless. There were flowers in vases on every surface; Jack never failed to bring her flowers, even when she was too ill or too drugged to see them. Flowers were only the smallest token of his feelings, but they were a constant one. Today Joy was sitting up against her pillows and her eyes were bright. True, she was still very weak, but her spirits were higher than Jack had seen them since her hospitalization. To Lewis it seemed that Joy now sat among her flowers like a rose, and when she saw Jack again, she positively blossomed.

"You won't believe this," smiled Joy happily. "Judy, she's the sister, she's been asking my advice about her love life. Me! She's been going out with this boy for two years. Will he marry her? How far should she let him go without them being at least engaged? I'm telling you, I'm almost sick with excitement. She's seeing him again on Saturday."

"It strikes me you're rather better," Jack said quietly.

Joy placed a finger to her lips and cast her eyes up to the ceiling. "Shh! We have to pretend we haven't noticed, or He'll take it away." It was that most ancient superstition, common to the Jews, the Chinese, the Athenians, among others. Don't say things are going well; don't look too happy. It's unlucky. The gods don't like it. The gods tend to punish humans when things are going too well for them.

Recognizing the superstition, Jack smiled. "So what advice did you give her?"

Joy's eyes sparkled with mischief. "I said, give him enough to make him want the rest, then nothing till he pays up."

"Poor fellow, he hasn't a chance," laughed Lewis, filled with delight at Joy's happy meddling.

"Speaking of Him, how did you square it?" She lifted one eyebrow up toward the ceiling and Heaven.

"Marrying you?" Jack had been waiting for just such a question. He knew that if she had the strength to ask it, Joy wouldn't miss the chance. How could she? There he was, on record more than once, in print and on the BBC, as the defender of the sanctity of marriage until death, and now here he was married to a divorced woman. Had C. S. Lewis compromised his beliefs in order to marry the woman he loved? How would he wriggle out of this one?

"Yes. I'm very curious."

Lewis took the question quite literally. "I did think about it, yes. The argument I put to myself went like this: I want to marry Joy, but if she's married to someone else, I can't. Whatever a divorce court decrees, marriage is indissoluble in the eyes of God. But your husband had been married before. If marriage is indissoluble, he's still married to his first wife. If he's still married to his first wife, he can't have married you. Not in the eyes of God. If he didn't marry you, you're unmarried, and free to marry me."

Joy nodded judiciously. "I can't see what's wrong with that."

"Nor me."

A pretty nursing sister came in pushing a trolley on which were medications, Joy's among them. Joy gestured very slightly with her head, but the significant look in her eye told Lewis plainly that this was Judy, the nurse with boyfriend trouble. It was time for him to go; Joy would soon be lost to him in the abyss of a medicated sleep. He stood up and kissed her goodbye.

"Back tomorrow." Then he turned to Judy. "Good luck on Saturday," he said.

When he left the hospital, there was lightness in Jack Lewis's step. The doctor had held out very little hope, but between very little hope and no hope at all lay a wide ocean of possibility on which Jack Lewis could navigate.

The news of Lewis's wife's apparent improvement spread quickly round the senior common room. The dons discussed it among themselves as they sipped their preprandial sherries, smoothed their robes, and prepared to go in to dinner.

At Oxford, there is no tradition of ambling into the dining hall wearing an old tweed jacket and taking one's seat at the high table whenever one choses, or feels hungry. No, the professors at Magdalen College all march in together, as a procession, in order of their seniority or position, with the president in the lead, and all of them dressed in their traditional black academic gowns. In a kind of minipageant, the dons come out of the common room, cross a roof walkway that leads to the dining hall, make their way through a little doorway into the brightly lighted hall, and take their places solemnly in front of the great carved screen. Only then may dinner be served to the undergraduates on the benches below. The daily pageantry lends a genuinely ancient authority to roasted mutton and Brussels sprouts.

"Excellent news. It appears that Mrs. Gresham is not to die after all," Harry Harrington told Christopher Riley and Rupert Parrish as they all put on their gowns.

"That is good news," agreed Riley.

"I think we should be calling her Mrs. Lewis, shouldn't we?" suggested Parrish.

"If she does recover, we shall chalk it up as a

victory for the power of prayer," the chaplain smiled.

I should think we could chalk it up to the power of radiation therapy, thought Christopher Riley. Aloud, he said, with a mocking lift of his eyebrow, "I've never quite understood about prayer. Does God intervene in the world only when He's asked?"

"It has been known," the Reverend Harrington retorted a bit stiffly. He was sensitive on the subjects of answered prayers and miracles, both of which were controversial, even among dedicated Christians. It took a special kind of believer to accept miracles, one with a pure and childlike innocence, which described the chaplain perfectly.

"And what are the qualifications for divine aid?" purred Riley. He loved getting the chaplain's goat, even though Harrington was easy prey. "Merit? Intense suffering? Persistent prayer? I mean, how does He choose?"

"I hardly think this is the time or the place for a theological argument." The Reverend Harry Harrington hoped this would put a stop to Riley's sardonic atheistic comments, although in his heart he knew better. Riley was only just getting warmed up.

"And if God knows what is best for us anyway, why do we need to ask? Doesn't He know already?"

The chaplain was saved from Riley's further

torments by the hurried appearance of Jack Lewis, who arrived late, and was struggling to get into his gown. "Jack. What news?"

"Good news, I think. Yes, good news."

"I'm very glad, Jack," smiled Riley. Even the severe portraits of former presidents and celebrated scholars hanging in their gilded frames on the wood-paneled walls seemed to be smiling.

"Christopher can scoff," said Harrington, "but I know how hard you've been praying, Jack. And now God is answering your prayer."

Lewis smoothed out the creases in his gown and took his place in the forming line. He spoke very seriously. "That's not why I pray, Harry. I pray because I can't help myself. I pray because I'm helpless. I pray because the need flows out of me all the time, waking and sleeping. It doesn't change God. It changes me."

"There's your answer, Christopher," laughed Rupert Parrish.

"That's the first sensible thing I've ever heard anybody say on the subject," ceded Riley.

The procession got under way, and conversation came to a halt. Jack Lewis walked along with his fellow dons, but his thoughts were not on the impending meal. His thoughts were where they always were these days. In London, in a small room filled with flowers, his thoughts came to rest on a white hospital bed, and the sweet-faced woman who was his wife, whom he loved with all his heart.

The following day, when Lewis took the London train, his brother Warnie came with him. As they walked down the long corridor to Jack's room, Dr. Craig was just coming out. "How is she, Doctor?" asked Jack.

The doctor tried to hide a smile, but failed. "Well, I think you should see for yourself."

Jack hurried past him into Joy's room, while Warnie stood watching in the doorway. The bed was empty. Joy—miracle of miracles—was out of bed, standing supported by two crutches, with Judy, the nursing sister, at her side, just in case. When Joy saw Jack and Warnie, her face lit up happily.

"Watch me, everybody." Clutching the crutches awkwardly, Joy managed to take a single step forward, then stopped, waiting for applause.

"Can you do more?" asked Lewis, applauding.

"A little. Come nearer."

Lewis took a few steps toward his wife, then stopped. Joy took a deep breath, gauging the distance between them. Then, at an uneven pace, she set off clumsily on her crutches and took the few steps necessary to fall into her husband's arms.

Her breathing was heavy; trying to walk with those crutches was damned hard work! She looked up into Lewis's face.

"How'd I do?"

He hugged her tightly. "Not bad." With tears of happiness in his eyes, Jack turned to Dr. Craig. "Does she have to stay here?" he demanded.

"I see no reason why. So long as the remission continues." It was the first time the doctor had spoken the word "remission" out loud. Now it was official. Joy Lewis was in remission. The cancer had loosened its hold upon her . . . for now.

"Which is how long?" Lewis pressed the doctor for an answer. Dr. Craig glanced nervously at Joy. "You can speak openly," demanded Jack. "She does have an interest in the matter."

Dr. Craig considered his answer. He didn't want to spoil their present happiness, but in truth he was unable to hold out too much hope. "It could be months. It could be weeks."

"Why not years?" demanded Lewis ferociously.

Dr. Craig hesitated. "In such an advanced case, that would be . . . unusual."

"Right. We take what we can get." Jack looked down into Joy's eyes. "Would you like to come home?"

"Where's home, Jack?" asked Joy softly.

200

"Oxford. My house. Our house. You're my wife, remember?"

"Oh, yes, Jack. Please take me home."

"I'll make immediate arrangements. We'll go home the day after tomorrow."

There would be a great deal to do to get the house ready for Joy. How to make her comfortable? Electric fires, that was the ticket! Joy was always cold, and without central heating she'd suffer a chill even in mild weather. Warnie should go directly to Rogerson's the ironmonger and buy an electric fire for every room in the house, the luxury kind with three bars, four if they had them.

"Warnie . . ." began Jack, as they walked out of the hospital together.

Now here it came, the sentence that Major Warren Lewis had been dreading to hear ever since his brother's marriage. With Joy and Douglas in the house, The Kilns would be pretty full up. No more room for old Warnie. Well, there was nothing for it but to make the best of it. "No need to worry about me, Jack. I'll sort myself out," he said manfully.

"Sort yourself out? What do you mean?" Lewis was totally mystified.

"New digs. No problem." He was damned if he was going to be in the way.

Warnie moving out of The Kilns? Warnie in new

living quarters? A flat somewhere? Or, worse, a furnished bedsitter? What could he be thinking of? "Do you want to?" asked the astonished Lewis.

"As you wish, Jack." *No, of course I don't want to. The Kilns is my home, the only home I've known for more than twenty-five years. How can you suppose that I would willingly leave it? But it's your house, Jack. You bought it; you own it.*

"I don't wish. I absolutely do not wish." Jack said vehemently. Warnie leave The Kilns? Impossible! Life without his brother was unthinkable. And now he was needed even more than ever. Even so, Jack Lewis recognized the generous sacrifice that Warnie was willing to make, although to speak of it aloud would be an embarrassment to them both.

"Right you are," Warnie said mildly, but inside him was a feeling of intense relief, and he rejoiced without a word.

"That's settled then. Now, what I wanted to talk to you about was electric fires. For Joy, you know. She's always so cold. Still not used to our damp British climate, I'm afraid. Do you suppose that The Kilns dilapidated old wiring will be able to support them? All these power cuts by the Electricity Board."

Warnie thought about the problem. "Well, Jack," he said slowly, "if we switched them on only in one room at a time, and switched them off when Joy left the room, there would probably be no danger to the wiring. I think you're right. They'll keep Joy nice and warm. Better lay in an extra supply of coal for the fires, though."

"Good thought, Warnie. What ever would I do without you, old man? Now tell me, what would you think about rewiring The Kilns? Putting in all new points? Or perhaps we might go to central heating? Would it cost the earth, do you suppose?"

Ah, thought Warnie. *It is his dream that Joy is going to live forever. Poor chap.*

Two days later, Joy Lewis came home. It was a bright, clear day in early April, when the cool spring breezes bring a promise of future summer sunshine. Both Jack and Warnie accompanied her in the ambulance from London. When the ambulance pulled up to the front gate of The Kilns, Joy was transferred into a wheelchair, and handed down with as much care as if she were a fragile, precious gem, which to Jack she was. He had never thought to see this day, the day when he could bring his darling wife home to The Kilns. God's mercy was indeed infinite.

She looked radiant. Her hair had been brushed until it shone in the sunlight and her eyes were bright with happiness. Color blossomed in her cheeks and on her lips. Now that she was off her mind-destroying painkillers, Joy seemed to be her old bright self again. There was about her an air of good health, despite the wheelchair and despite the woolen carriage robe tucked around her legs. The wholesome air of Oxfordshire would do her good, of that Jack Lewis was convinced. And they'd all be looking after her. They'd be so good to Joy, all of them. Douglas and Warnie and Mrs. Young and even old Paxford. And he himself would never let her out of his sight. Cared for like this, how could Joy fail to get better?

The ambulance driver pushed the wheelchair up to the front door. Jack followed with Joy's suitcase, and Warnie went on ahead, to fling the door wide and hold it open. There was a welcoming committee of three—the housekeeper, Mrs. Young, Paxford, the old gardener, and, certainly the happiest of them all, Douglas. He could hardly believe that his mother was coming home—Douglas now thought of The Kilns as his home—even though he'd been waiting for this minute for what seemed to him an eternity.

For more than an hour, he'd been standing by the window of the second floor landing, waiting for the first sign of the ambulance, then watching it arrive, seeing his mother as the wheelchair bumped and rattled her along the path toward the house. A wheelchair! Somehow, Douglas had never pictured his vital and active mother as somebody sitting in a wheelchair. The woman in the chair was almost a stranger to him, so Douglas didn't come down the stairs right away, but watched Joy's homecoming from upstairs on the landing. It was only when he saw his mother looking around for him so eagerly that he started slowly down the steps.

As soon as she was inside the door, Joy looked around for Douglas. When she saw him coming shyly down the stairs, her smile grew broader, and she held her arms outwide. Uttering a small cry, the boy ran forward and threw himself against her chest. Hugging him, Joy thought she'd never been so happy in her life. She was loved by a good man and she adored him in return. She felt herself blessed by God's mercy after all. Feeling better, going home, now here with Douglas in her arms, Joy had been given her discount.

"I've missed you so much, darling," she whispered into her son's soft hair.

"Me, too, Mommy."

"There, Douglas, don't you tire out your mam. You'll have plenty of chances to be with her from now on." In a firm but kindly way Mrs. Young disentangled the boy. "Shall we go in and make the tea? I'll wager your mam could use a cup."

As the lad and the housekeeper headed for the

kitchen, old Paxford shuffled forward in his heavy, clumsy boots with a bunch of spring flowers—narcissi and tulips, and hyacinths mingled with a few stems of purple lilac. "Might as well pick them, I thought," the old fellow said gruffly, presenting them to Joy. "They would have died anyhow."

Joy accepted the fragrant flowers with a grateful smile. "Thank you, Paxford. They're lovely."

"Tell *him*," sniffed Paxford, meaning Jack Lewis. "He never notices." His respects paid to the new missus, he took himself and his heavy boots back to his garden.

Joy rested downstairs on the drawing room sofa for most of the afternoon. She felt rather like that literary invalid Elizabeth Barrett, wrapped in a shawl, waiting for her poet/lover Robert Browning to pay a call. Sleeping sometimes, awake and thinking at other times, Joy was grateful for the privacy and for the warmly glowing bars of the new electric fire in the drawing room. For the first time since she had come to England, she felt warm enough. Later, there was another heater in the dining room, too, and Joy's chair was placed closest to it. Joy recognized the thought and love that went into all these little electric heaters, but she said nothing, not wishing to embarrass Jack or Warnie by a reference to their generosity.

Dinner was convivial, perhaps the most cheerful meal ever eaten at that table. Paxford's little bouquet had the place of honor in the center of the table, where it spread its perfume into the air, and long wax tapers burned in heavy silver candlesticks. Out of deference to Joy, who was not allowed wine, only cider was served, yet Warnie never complained. He drank his cider with a glad heart, enjoying the sight of his extended family around the table, and knowing he was an important member of that family.

Douglas's chair was next to Joy's, and all during the meal he would reach out and touch her lightly, as though checking to see that she was real and not merely some fantasy born of his wishful thinking. Watching them, Jack Lewis smiled inwardly, but he had the impulse to do the same thing himself.

Joy ate well, with good appetite, even accepting a second helping of roly-poly for dessert, to Mrs. Young's great satisfaction. As Warnie and Douglas helped to clear away the dishes, Jack went behind Joy's chair and pulled it out gently. With a great effort, she stood up and leaned all her weight backward against him, using him as a crutch. Together, with Jack behind Joy, propelling her forward, they took a step or two in the direction of the door.

"Not bad?" Joy asked proudly.

"Not bad," he smiled. They took another step together, then another. It was an enormous effort for both of them, each step a fresh obstacle to be surmounted. Although she was a slender woman, and since her illness had lost a great deal of weight, Joy couldn't bear any of her own weight on her cancerous leg. Lewis had to do it all, but he did it with gladness. Anything he could do for Joy made him happy.

"Now, I don't want to hear any talk of miracles," cautioned Jack with a smile.

"Why not?" Joy demanded indignantly. "It's a miracle to me. You leave my miracles alone."

"You were alive before," he murmured softly. "I wasn't."

"What are you talking about?"

Jack Lewis stopped, and holding Joy tightly, turned her around so that they could look into each other's eyes. His face was very serious. "I started living when I started loving you, Joy. That makes me only a few months old."

Trembling with emotion, Joy shut her eyes. It was the most beautiful thing anybody had ever said to her.

N I N E

May Day

Joy's first day home had been long, event-filled, emotional, and exhausting, and everyone was ready for bed early. But neither Douglas nor Joy could think about sleep until they had spent their own private time together, as in the old days. It had been a very long time since Joy had tucked her son into bed and kissed him good night. So much had happened to both of them in the last months that they would need time to become reacquainted. Jack was very careful not to intrude on them, although he had to be ready nearby in case Joy should have need of him. So he stood on the landing, across the hall from the door of Douglas's bedroom, contemplating the night sky and the vivid constellations of stars through the landing window, in the very same spot where Douglas had stood earlier today as he watched his mother come home in a wheelchair.

Jack didn't hear the soft words that mother and

son were speaking to each other, Joy sitting on the edge of Douglas's bed, caressing the boy's hair. He made no attempt to overhear, but even so he was very conscious of the lovely picture they made in the lamplight, a little boy and his mum, the two of them teamed up against the rest of the world, partners, friends. His own memory filled up with poignant recollections of his own mother, dead now almost fifty years, and of how much he'd loved her and needed her. Now it seemed he needed only God and Joy. And Joy needed him. What a blessed necessity! To be of prime importance to someone you love so much. Lewis's heart was so full of emotion it threatened to spill over into tears.

His life had been altered so dramatically in such a short span of time! Jack Lewis, who had never once missed the touch of a woman's hand since the death of his mother, who defined love as that which was given to and received from God Almighty, who distanced himself from his fellow man and especially from his fellow woman, this same Jack Lewis was now head over heels in love! What a turnaround! In a mere matter of months the old bachelor, set in his ways, living only for himself, had become a doting husband and even in some sense a father!

For Lewis had come to love Douglas Gresham as a son, rejoicing in the many similar characteristics the two of them shared. Bookish and introspective, shy, intelligent, and thoughtful, young Douglas was mature beyond his years, questioning, a truth seeker, yet at the same time a dreamer. Lewis at Douglas's age had been very much like this boy, spending many hours alone, reading and imagining. Forever asking questions. Always peeping around corners to see what would come next, always hoping that it would be something fantastical and magical. Looking now at Douglas, Jack saw himself mirrored as he used to be more than forty years ago. He understood what the boy must be suffering now, that mixture of gladness for Joy's presence and bitter fear for her future and his. With Douglas Jack shared the identical feelings.

In loving Joy, in making her his wife, Jack knew that he had given himself the greatest gift of all, the gift of expressing love and living in love for another. Isn't that what Christ taught? Love one another? How was it possible he hadn't seen it for so many years? The basic precept of Christian life, there under his nose all this while. Oh, heavens, thought Jack as he stared out into the star-filled night, how many times I lectured on that very subject, love, and how many words I penned on love's behalf, and all the while I hadn't the faintest clue what the hell I was talking about. How stupidly blind I used to be! Thank you, God, for making me a bit less ignorant. And thank you, Joy, for making it come to pass.

And then, as he did so often, Jack Lewis prayed. This time his prayers were filled with gratitude, not anguish. He had hoped, and his hopes had been fulfilled. Joy was better, and Joy was home. Since God had already passed a kind of miracle, surely He could pass another, and let her live!

Joy gave her son one last soft kiss, and Douglas settled down for sleep. "Ready, Jack," she called.

Entering Douglas's room, Lewis helped her to her feet and, with Joy leaning on him, they walked slowly into the bedroom down the hall. Jack's bedroom. Now it would be Joy's bedroom, too. Jack Lewis found the thought so unfamiliar that it was a bit intimidating.

"Let me just sit down for a moment, Jack. I need a lot of pauses." Joy winced in pain, and looked pale. Lewis bent over her anxiously.

"I think it might be better if I lie down."

Tenderly, Jack helped his wife fully onto the bed, lifting her legs very gently and making sure they were straight. Gratefully, Joy lay back on the pillows. "That's better, darling," she sighed.

Jack brought blankets to wrap around Joy's shoulders and body, and an extra pillow to prop under her head. "As I look at this room, it strikes me it is a bit on the Spartan side," he said with an anxious glance at his wife.

Joy took a long look around the room, seeing a man's simple living quarters. Piles of books and magazines which accumulated in every room that Jack inhabited, a utilitarian reading light by the bed, an ashtray. Everything done in drab, neutral colors, with worn furniture, faded paint, and very old wallpaper beginning to peel at the corners. Jack had obviously been sleeping in a single bed, because now a second single bed had been brought in and pushed together with the first. The beds didn't match each other and neither did their bedclothes.

But it was clean, and as tidy as Mrs. Young could make it, considering the habits of the room's occupant. Joy appreciated the sharp contrast between this shabby, lived-in bedroom with its familiar furniture and books and the charming vase of garden flowers placed on the dresser just for her, and the institutional, antiseptic hospital room in which Joy had spent so many painful days and agonized nights. Compared with that, this room was paradise. Another brand-new electric fire stood on the floor, warming the area of the bed that would be hers. How thoughtful Jack was, how caring and loving. Joy felt an upsurge of a feeling close to adoration for this wonderful, brilliant, thoughtful man she'd married.

Most important of all, this was Jack's own bedroom, his *sanctum sanctorum,* yet he was prepared to share it with her as husband and wife.

"It's exactly all right, Jack." And she meant it.

He came and sat beside her on the bed, Joy stretching out to ease her aching bones. She lifted his hand to her lips and kissed it. "Thank you, my love."

"What for?"

"All of it."

Jack smiled at her, then looked critically around the room. It was so familiar to him that he hadn't really noticed anything about it in years. It was comfortable; it suited Jack's needs; he never expected more of it. Now all of a sudden the room looked outdated and cheerless. Would his wife be comfortable here? Why hadn't he noticed that the wallpaper was faded and peeling? Why hadn't he thought to get new curtains before Joy came home? The old ones suddenly appeared to him as drab and quite shabby. And pillows. He should have bought a few bright pillows to scatter about. The homely touch. No, he was absolutely hopeless at things like this, and Warnie wasn't much help in this department. He ought to have consulted Mrs. Young. Women had an instinctive understanding of such matters. "Now that I look at this room, it

214

strikes me it's a little on the Spartan side," he fretted.

"How long has it been your room?" asked Joy.

Lewis thought. "Twenty-five years. More, I suppose."

"Ever shared it with anyone else?" She was teasing, yet not entirely. Joy was pretty sure that Jack had enjoyed much less experience in matters of the heart than she herself had in days gone by. Joy was a free spirit, but C. S. Lewis, author and Christian scholar, could scarcely be described as that. Still, appearances were often deceiving. . . . Jack was a good-looking and famous man. . . . Women were often aggressive. . . .

Jack shook his head. He had never shared this room with another person, had never even considered it. In his youth he'd been a passionate, lusty boy, but for decades he'd disciplined his passions, turning them into mental exercises that resulted in yet another book, yet another lecture. C. S. Lewis's life was a life of the mind. Now this, like everything else, was going to change.

Instinctively, Joy sensed something of what her husband was thinking and feeling. This was all new to him. "Feel strange?" she asked him softly.

Jack nodded. "I'm not entirely sure of the procedure," he confessed.

"What do you usually do when you go to bed?"

215

"Very much what you'd expect." He felt a bit embarrassed in talking about going to bed, even with his wife.

"No, tell me," Joy insisted. "You come in the door. What then?"

"I draw the curtains." He went to the windows and drew the curtains across the panes. Jack thought a second. "Then I get out my pajamas."

"Where from?"

"Under the pillow." To prove it, he pulled a pair of folded pajamas out from under his pillow, which made Joy smile. It was somehow touching to see Jack's nightclothes, touching, sweet, and very intimate.

"Of course. Then what?"

Jack went over the list in his memory, ticking the items off one by one. "Hang my clothes over the chair. Clean my teeth. Wash. Turn back the bedclothes. Kneel by the bed. Pray. Get into bed."

"Like a little boy," Joy said fondly. She could easily picture it, the familiar routine he'd developed over the years, the habits of a lifetime. Familiar habits that must have brought him comfort and security.

"Is it?"

She nodded. "What next?"

"Then I go to sleep."

"On your back or your side?"

"On my side."

"Show me."

Lewis stretched out next to Joy, facing her. She turned on her side to face him. Putting out one arm, she drew her husband closer. He shifted himself so he fitted into her arms, and so they lay cuddled together, face-to-face, blue eyes looking into dark gray eyes.

"You do everything just the way you always do, Jack," whispered Joy with infinite love in her voice. "Only when you get to the last bit, I'll be here, too." She sighed happily and nestled closer, tucking her head under his chin. "That's the procedure."

He tightened his arms around her gratefully. His wife, his dear beloved, was home. God had given them this much, and Jack Lewis prayed that God would grant them the even more precious gift of time.

Joy came home to The Kilns in the first week of April. As Jack had hoped, just being out of the hospital and among the people who loved her had worked a special kind of healing. All of them at The Kilns treated her not as an invalid, but as somebody infinitely rare and precious, a person to be cherished. Under their loving care, Joy Lewis's strength expanded like a rose growing in sunshine.

It seemed that day by day she became stronger. By mid-April she was so proficient on the crutches that she rarely had to lean on Jack or Warnie. By the third week in April, she had virtually abandoned one of the crutches and walked with the support of a single crutch.

Of course, she and Jack couldn't walk far. A few turns around the front garden and Joy had to sit down, breathless. Nevertheless, she was out of doors, where she could see the blue sky, smell Paxford's beautiful flowers, and feel the sun and the wind on her face. It was freedom, more than they could possibly have hoped for. Warnie took it upon himself to see to it that sturdy chairs were placed at convenient intervals around the garden, so that Joy would have a seat available whenever she couldn't stand up a moment more.

Another big change at The Kilns. Jack and Warnie hadn't driven an automobile since before the war, but now Jack determined to buy one so that he could take Joy out for drives. It was also foolish, he said, to live outside Oxford and not to keep a car in case of emergencies. And, moreover, he could afford it. After all, he was a bestselling author whose royalty checks were frequent and generous. And they'd lived so simply for all these years that very little of it got spent, and the money was simply accruing interest.

Together with Warnie, Jack went to several motor showrooms in town, looking at one model after another, until the final decision came down to an Austin sedan or a Humber. The Humber cost hundreds of pounds more than the Austin, but it was more luxurious, and Jack Lewis wanted Joy to have every luxury. Both Joy and Warnie protested the extra expense was madness, but what decided Jack in the end to buy the Austin was the fact that it was available immediately, while the would-be Humber purchaser's name would have to go on a waiting list.

In the Austin, the four of them—Jack, Joy, Warnie, and Douglas—motored happily around Oxfordshire, eating sandwiches packed by Mrs. Young or lunching at country inns and visiting sights of interest, particularly churches and cathedrals. Joy's favorite was a simple stone ninth century church they found tucked away on a back road. Low-ceilinged and made of crudely dressed stones, with an altar carved of walnut wood and decorated with simple wildflower offerings, it exuded so ancient a faith that Jack was immediately enraptured.

"This church was standing here when the Vikings came raiding," he whispered reverently as they stood in the nave and looked around them. "It was old in the Middle Ages, and ancient when

Chaucer penned his verses and Shakespeare wrote his plays. This little Church has seen civil wars between the White Rose and the Red, between Roundhead and Cavalier, it's been through Napoleonic wars, two world wars, and Heaven knows how many other armed conflicts. This church is a living piece of history, a testament to humanity's enduring faith in God."

"Not to mention," Joy whispered back, "that it's cute as a button."

Which made her husband laugh out loud in church, a first.

When it came to anything pertaining to her husband, Joy had virtual total recall. She remembered every word that Jack Lewis had ever spoken to her. As the first day of May approached, she reminded him of what he'd told her the first time they'd met. Joy, Warnie, and Jack had climbed to the top of the Magdalen College bell tower and were standing there, looking down over the campus, the river Cherwell and Magdalen Bridge.

At dawn, he'd said, "On the first of May every year, the choristers from the choir school stand up here and sing to the rising sun. I'm told they draw quite a crowd."

"What do they sing?" Joy had asked eagerly.

"I can't say I've ever risen early enough to hear them."

220

"Why not? It sounds wonderful." She now remembered how she imagined the choristers in their pristine robes, hailing the dawn while their high pure voices chanted an anthem of praise to the rising sun. Standing on the platform of the high bell tower, Joy had felt as though she were actually there in the damp chill of six o'clock of an English May morning, the stars still out, the sky still almost black, but in the east the first pink trail of dawn heralding the sunrise. She had also imagined the dons in their black gowns and scarlet hoods, but C. S. Lewis was not among them.

Lewis had shrugged. "I don't really go in for seeing the sights."

It had struck Joy then that there must be a streak of snobbishness in this man; how could he live and work so close to something so beautiful and historical and never even bother to go and see it, merely because it smacked of tourism? Now that she knew him so much better, she understood his shrinking from crowded places, but even so, she was determined to attend the May Day morning services this year, and equally determined that Jack should share them with her.

There was nothing that Joy could ask for that Jack would not willingly give. For years, he had avoided the May Day ceremonies not only because they drew crowds of noisy tourists but because of their pagan origins, as Druidic in nature as Stonehenge. The godless human, ignorant of Christ's divine love, hailing the rising sun as his god. Surely in the twentieth century mankind should have learned better than to celebrate heathen feast days. But if his beloved wife wanted to hear the choristers on May Day morning, Jack Lewis could not and would not deny her that pleasure.

Accordingly, on the morning of the first of May, an alarm clock woke Jack and Joy two hours before sunrise. While Joy got herself ready, Jack prepared a thermos of hot tea to take along. He packed the boot of the Austin with blankets and helped Joy into the auto. They drove down Headington Hill into Oxford, and parked the car not far from the underside of the Magdalen Bridge. Then, with Joy leaning on her single crutch, they made their way slowly to the banks of the Cherwell, under the bridge, where they found a good vantage point for viewing the ceremony.

It was some ten minutes before six in the morning and still dark and cold. The sky glittered with the icy points of a trillion stars, while below, the river was misted over. Even so, the bridge was already crowded with spectators, and the river was filled with punts, low open boats filled with male and female students, many of them carrying lit torches. Joy shivered in her warm coat and muffler, and Jack held the steaming thermos cup of tea up for her to sip from. The riverbanks were covered by crowds of tourists and townsfolk from Oxford, many with cameras hung round their necks, all with their eyes turned to the east, where the sun was due to rise in only a few minutes. On the High Street, all traffic had been stopped, and motorists were standing next to their cars, also peering eastward. Jack was struck by how quiet it was; with hundreds of people gathered here to watch the sunrise on May Day, you'd expect a lot of rowdy noise, yet the spectators were surprisingly quiet.

On the crenellated parapet of the bell tower stood the college choristers, shivering in their white-and-gold robes. They, too, were waiting for the sun to show its face. Then, as this little world held its breath, in the east the first Aurora pink rays broke through the night's blackness. The glow became longer, wider, deeper, and orange-and-gold streaks were added to the pink. Suddenly, the rounded shape of the sun began to peep over the edge of the world. With one sweet voice, the choristers broke into song, saluting the May Day morning. First they sang in Latin, then in Old English. The soloist's treble voice rose higher than the others, pure and heartbreakingly sweet.

> *Sumer is icumen in,* they sang,
> *Lhude sing cuccu!*
> *Groweth sed, and bloweth med,*
> *And springeth the wude nu—*
> *Sing cuccu!*

The ancient English song, seven hundred years old, rose faintly but clearly in the morning air, filling the silence with the wonder of the world made new. Only four lines long, it took but a moment to be heard, and then the chant disappeared in a dying fall of notes. The sun began its climb into the heavens, and its rays fell across the ancient stones of Oxford, and across the faces of the singing choristers, staining them with gold.

A great cheer went up, and the party began. From the punts on the river came a loud popping of champagne corks and the cries of pretty girls calling up to the boys on Magdalen Bridge. On the bridge itself, several young men dove into the Chertwell and splashed happily toward the boats. On shore, there was the continual explosion of flashbulbs as the delighted tourists captured the moment on film. Hawkers of refreshments began to shout their wares.

Leaning on her husband, Joy stood watching, enchanted by the exuberance of it all and still enraptured by the glorious voices of the chorus.

She remembered the May Days of her younger years, when she was a Party member. She recalled that, while the Soviet armies paraded in Red Square, in New York City battalions of serious-faced workers in dark cloth caps marched down Broadway to Union Square, carrying red banners. The labor union organizers and the wobblies; the folk singers with their guitars and their songs of protest, the ordinary working stiffs, all paraded to show their solidarity with the workers of the world. The marchers were surrounded on all sides by mounted policemen, who were called out every year in force to make sure the Bolshies and the anarchists didn't start any trouble.

Once arrived at Union Square, the marchers would mass quietly, listening raptly to the inflammatory Communist speakers who promised them the coming workers' paradise, a worldwide fraternity of laboring men and women who would own the means of production and throw out the bosses and the fat cats and put an end to the exploitation of the poor and downtrodden. Then the folk singers would tune up their banjos and guitars, and all of them would sing out the robust ballads of the hard life of the farmer and the miner. On many a May Day, Joy Davidman had raised her voice in "The Internationale" with her fellow workers and called them "comrade."

Now her life had come full circle, and she was again listening to music on May Day. But how different it all was! Now her true comrade was this marvelous man standing beside her, and her faith in the Party had long ago disappeared, along with her youthful wrongheadedness, to be replaced by a mature but simple faith in God. Joy looked up at Jack, and was both amused and touched to see that he was smiling. Jack, too, had been moved by the beauty of the singing and its symbolic welcome of the sun's increase into summer. She nudged him.

"Admit it; you're glad I made you come," Joy said.

Lewis smiled his assent. "It's pagan, and it's vulgar, and it's all faintly silly, but it works."

Joy tucked her hand into Jack's arm and smiled up at him. "Sunrise always works," she said, as the bells of the Oxford churches began to ring and ring.

Joy was sitting in the downstairs study, at Jack's desk, with Douglas sharing the chair with her. They were studying the framed watercolor of the rustic valley hanging on the study wall. Douglas was typing slowly, one finger at a time, writing his description of the picture. Joy had seen it many times, but she hadn't really looked at it since the first time. Now she concentrated on it, her eyes narrowing. "Jack, where did you say this Golden Valley was?" she asked thoughtfully.

Lewis came in from the garden. "Somewhere in Herefordshire, I believe."

She kissed Douglas and the boy left the room. "Do you think it still looks the same?" asked Joy.

Lewis thought of the changes in the British landscape over the last ten years, the hideous housing blocks and council flats, the glass-and-steel office buildings and industrial parks that had mushroomed up to spoil the rural look of the nation. "I very much doubt it," he said.

Joy couldn't take her eyes off the picture. "You thought it was Heaven, didn't you?"

"I was only a child," Jack defended himself.

"Let's go and look for it, Jack," she said suddenly. "We haven't had a honeymoon."

Jack stared at his wife, astonished. Where on earth had she got hold of an idea that? Yet, the idea was intriguing. "Are you up to traveling?"

"It's not so far, is it?"

Lewis's brow creased. "I don't really know. Where would we stay?"

"Some little country hotel."

Jack shook his head, laughing. "I truly believe that if I had to go into a hotel with a woman and sign the register, I'd blush."

"Then I'll sign the register," said Joy. "Mr. and

Mrs. Joy Davidman Gresham Lewis." And so it was settled.

They set out for Herefordshire in the Austin on a bright morning in late May. The plan was to drive to Cheltenham and spend the night in one of those grand old hotels that dot the promenade, where retired military men and their plump wives sit playing bridge and drinking tea. From there, they would motor through the Vale of Evesham, a garden spot that Jack was particularly eager for Joy to see; after lunch in Evesham, it was an easy drive across to Hereford, near the Welsh border. Outside Hereford, they would stay in a country hotel as Joy had suggested, and the following day begin their quixotic search for the heavenly Golden Valley of Jack's nursery engraving.

The hotel in Cheltenham was everything a British hotel ought to be—traditional, with excellent service, large, bright warm rooms, overstuffed chairs covered in flowered cretonne, a reading room stocked with crested writing paper and a selection of international newspapers, and a grand dining room that served up rich teas, five-course dinners, and enormous breakfasts of kippers, kedgeree, curried chicken, shirred eggs, thick-cut rashers of country bacon, tiny quail, large sausages, very hot toast oozing with butter, and heavy cream for the strong Indian tea.

"I could spend a week here," purred Joy, drying her hair with one of the wide, thick towels that were so generously provided. "Two weeks, if you twisted my arm."

"Would you like to? We're in no hurry," offered Jack.

"Don't tempt me. No, I'd like to press on and find our valley."

After a large breakfast, they drove on to Evesham, the market basket of England, where Jack purchased a large basket of fragrant, freshly picked strawberries plump with juice and smelling of sunshine. Joy held the basket in her lap, and they munched on them when lunchtime rolled around, so they wouldn't have to stop for a meal. Seeing Joy's lips stained scarlet by the berry juice, Jack grinned broadly.

Joy caught the smile out of the corner of her eye and grinned back.

"Happy?" he asked.

"Yes," she said simply.

"What kind of happy?"

"Just happy." *Just sunshine happy and strawberry happy and being with you happy and being alive at all happy.*

"Shall I tell you my kind of happy?" asked Lewis.

Joy clapped her forehead. "Stupid! I always forget. When you ask a question, it means you've got the answer waiting. Sure, go ahead. Tell me."

Jack pretended to be insulted. "No. I'm not telling you now."

"Oh, come on." She gave him a nudge in his ribs.

"No." He chose to play miffed.

"What do I have to do? Go to the lecture?"

"Yes. And buy the book."

Jack had booked them into The Swan, a large and rather elegant half-timbered Tudor hotel built with weathered brick, with irregular steps and a sizable kitchen garden out front. As they drove up the long driveway, Joy chuckled.

"Well, it's a hotel, and it's in the country." But this imposing structure was hardly the quaint old country inn she'd imagined.

The room they'd reserved was on the second floor, as Jack had specified, so that Joy would not be faced with climbing many stairs. In the grate, a fire was already burning, as Jack had insisted, and the room was toasty warm. It was furnished charmingly with a wide antique bed boasting tall carved bedposts and flowered linen curtains, and a wide mahogany wardrobe not unlike the one that Jack had made famous in his Narnia novels.

From the tall, deep windows one could see a broad view of lush green parkland. Joy made her way to one of the large windows—she was walking with two sticks now, in place of the crutch—and looked out with pleasure on a pastoral landscape of pleasant meadows and grazing sheep.

"Will it do?" Lewis asked.

"It's beautiful, Jack."

"Well, I must say, you seem to have survived the journey."

"I could do with a drink," said Joy. "Do they have room service?"

"Room service. I used to think that room service was saying prayers in bed."

She laughed. "You can order some prayers if you want. I will take a gin-and-tonic."

"What, now?"

"Sure. Why not?"

Looking dubious, Jack headed for the door.

"Honey," Joy called after him.

"What?"

"You can use the telephone."

Slightly embarrassed, Jack picked up the phone. Calling room service was not a concept he was familiar with, as Joy noted with amusement. "Hallo? This is Mr. Lewis, in room . . . I'm afraid I've forgotten the room number, and I'm inside it, if you see what I mean. Oh, is it? Very good. We'd like some drinks in our room, if that's possible. Ah, wonderful. A gin-and-tonic, and a . . . a . . ."

Jack drew a blank, he couldn't for the life of him think of what to order for himself. "And a gin-and-tonic. Two gin-and-tonics. Two gins-and-tonic, I should say. Thank you." When he hung the phone up, there were beads of perspiration on his brow from the effort.

"You don't like gin," Joy pointed out dryly.

"I'm afraid I panicked," he confessed, and so was created one more amusing memory for the two of them to store up.

The following morning, right after breakfast, Joy and Jack set out on their quest.

But where to begin? "The Golden Valley runs from here, to here, along the river Dore. Let me show you on the map." The hotel receptionist's manicured finger traced a line on Lewis's Ordonnance Survey map of Herefordshire.

"Why Golden?" asked Lewis.

"It's a mistake, really," said the receptionist. "The Welsh for water is *dwr*, which sounds like *d'or*, the French for golden. It's not Golden at all, actually. It's wet." Hearing this, Joy burst out laughing.

Hilarious as the error was, it was too late to back out now, having come this far. Besides, Joy had no intention of letting her husband back out. What they had come to find had too much symbolic meaning for Jack, whether golden or merely wet.

"And where can one get a view of the valley?" asked Lewis.

The receptionist consulted the map again. "I should go along here, to the junction here, and turn left up this little road. That'll take you up into the hills."

On the map it didn't look very far, but it was actually a long drive, because the distance was hardly as the crow flies. The country roads were narrow, and wound around themselves, so that they backtracked on a number of occasions. Once or twice, Jack was forced to stop the car and let a herd of slow-moving cattle cross the road ahead of them. Everywhere they drove, they kept looking out for the famous Golden Valley, but never caught sight of it. The sun had reached its zenith and was starting on its decline to the west, and still they drove on. Long shadows of linden trees made bars of darkness across the road, and still they journeyed.

"I don't know why we're doing this," grumbled Lewis, even though they were having a wonderful time and he was enjoying himself hugely. He had never had Joy all to himself for so long a time before this; always, Douglas and usually, Warnie were around.

"Yes, you do."

"It won't be the same. It's bound to have been spoilt."

Suddenly, Joy caught a glimpse of a farming valley from the car window. "That's it," she called out in excitement. "No, I'm wrong. The valley runs east-west, doesn't it?"

"I've no idea," Jack confessed. Navigation had never been his strong suit. All he could do was follow the line on the map and hope for the best.

They drove around a few more bends in the road. Still no sign of the valley. "You know we're there already, of course?" said Jack suddenly.

"Where?"

"There."

Then she realized what he was trying to tell her. That the two of them had their own private Golden Valley. They were in it together, shut away from everybody else. "Oh. There. Yes." It was only a word, that yes, but it spoke volumes of understanding. Joy's heart swelled with twofold exultation, with the renewed realization that not only was Jack making her happy, but that she herself was bringing happiness to him. It was Jack's loving her that was the true miracle.

T E N

The Deal

And then, just as they'd about given up hope of ever finding it, they rounded one last bend and there it was, spread out ahead of them and below, the Golden Valley, identical twin to the valley in Jack's picture. And it didn't look wet, but truly golden, because the slanting rays of the late afternoon sun were just now turning the valley to a molten yellow. Never mind what the Welsh word for water was, this valley was very definitely golden. And it was lush and unspoiled, no blocks of ugly flats, no factories, just a wide, clear landscape of farmland, farms, trees, hedgerows, and fields beside a long, rolling river, the Welsh Dore, or *dwr*. Joy clapped her hands in delighted triumph; in every detail it looked exactly like the watercolor hanging on the study wall of The Kilns. They had found Jack's heaven on earth.

"Well, well," exclaimed Lewis, truly surprised.

Jack pulled the car up to the shoulder of the road, and helped Joy out. There was a hillside path leading down to the valley past a large gray stone barn. Joy went ahead with her cane, Lewis following closely to make certain she was all right.

Side by side, together they walked through the high grass of the valley, with the rich scent of sun on dried grass filling up their senses, and lazy insects circling their heads. After a while, a late afternoon breeze struck up, bringing with it the threat of a much cooler evening. "A bit chilly for Heaven," remarked Jack, looking anxiously at Joy. She took cold so easily.

But Joy didn't appear to mind the chill. Her eyes were on the path. "Watch out for the stinging nettles," she called back. A few wet drops fell on Lewis's face. "Surely it isn't raining," he said, dismayed.

It was, of course, because England enjoys all four seasons almost every day, and now it was beginning to rain unpleasantly hard.

"Did you bring an umbrella?" called Joy over her shoulder.

"One doesn't expect rain in the afterlife," Jack retorted defensively.

A nearby stone barn seemed to offer the best chance for shelter, so they made for it as quickly as they could, with Joy hobbling on her sticks. The barn doors were wide open, and they ducked inside and looked around.

Hardly as luxurious as the hotel in Cheltenham, the old barn was at least dry. An important part of a working farm, and it was mostly used for the storage of vehicles and implements of farming. There were no animals here; the cows and pigs were stabled closer to the farmhouse. It was dark inside; the wooden rafters cast gloomy shadows over the barn floor. By an unspoken agreement, Joy and Jack did not penetrate into the gloom, but remained near the open doors. That way they could watch the rain and see the Golden Valley below turning to silver as it misted over. A wash of rain swept over the lower fields, and into the river Dore. Soon the landscape below them was indistinguishable.

Jack stood in the doorway, and Joy perched on the flatbed of a truck parked at the barn's entrance. Despite the chilly damp, Joy and Jack felt very cozy, and very much at peace. Sooner or later the rain would stop, and they'd be on their way, their search at an end. But it didn't much matter when. They were cold and they were hungry, but that didn't matter either.

Then Jack said softly, as though from very far away, "I don't want to be somewhere else anymore. I'm not waiting for anything new to happen. Not looking round the next corner, nor over the next hill. I'm here, now, and that's enough."

Joy looked up at him. "That's your kind of happy, is it?"

"Yes, yes it is."

His words gave Joy an incredible sense of security, and she reached up to kiss him. But this was the opportunity she had been waiting for; there was something on her mind, something she had to tell him. "It's not going to last, Jack," Joy said in a low tone.

Moving restlessly, Lewis turned away from her. "We shouldn't think about that now. Let's not spoil the time we have together."

Ever since she'd been released from the hospital, Joy had been troubled by Jack's refusal to face the truth. A remission was not a cure. She still had cancer, and it was likely to return at any time. Already, she had improved beyond anybody's expectations, but it could not go on forever. This was borrowed time, and they'd have to pay it back sooner or later. Joy felt strongly that she had to break through his denial. Unless Jack faced the truth together with her now, they would not be ready to face the end together later. Denial was for children and fools.

"Jack, it doesn't spoil it. It makes it real." Lewis kept his face averted, refusing to look at Joy.

"Let me just say it, before this rain stops, and we go back."

"What is there to say?" He turned pleading eyes on her, mutely begging her not to say what he knew she had to say.

"That I'm going to die."

He simply couldn't bear to hear her speak the words.

But Joy was insistent. "I want to be with you then, too, Jack. The only way I can do that is to talk to you about it now."

"I shall manage. Don't you worry about me," Jack said between clenched teeth.

Joy shook her head. "I think it can be better than that. Better than just managing. What I'm trying to say is that the pain, then, is part of the happiness, now."

It was the moment he had dreaded, when he'd be forced to acknowledge the bitter truth. Joy was right. This happiness could not last. It would be cut short long before they were both ready for it. The price they'd pay for their present closeness was that they would never grow old together, Joy and Jack. It was a price he'd agreed to pay when he married Joy in the eyes of God. He'd taken her for his wife, terminal cancer and all. "In sickness and in health . . . until death do you part."

"That's the deal," said Joy quietly.

Jack nodded, although he couldn't think how he would be able to endure it when the actual time came. He looked deeply into her eyes and she smiled at him, her lips trembling. Never in his life had he seen so much love in a face as he did now in Joy's. Silently, he moved toward her, gathering her up in his arms. When they kissed, it was with the deepest passion Jack Lewis had ever known. Her slim body trembled in his arms as Joy returned his kiss, caressing him with her pale hands. A million miles away from them, the Golden Valley disappeared into the rain.

The months passed, and Joy Lewis continued to hold her own. Jack arranged his schedule to spend as much time as possible with her, laying his writing aside, and refusing all speaking engagements. His only obligation was to look after Joy's comfort and happiness. But the time passed by so quickly! Balmy May turned to June; after Encaenia, Jack's classes were over for the summer, and this meant more hours spent with Joy, talking with Joy, sitting with Joy, reading out loud to Joy, driving her from place to place for lunch, or evensong, or some small treat like a visit to the Ashmolean and tea at the Randolph, the same hotel in which they'd first met.

In high summer, with the university almost

deserted, Jack took Joy around his beloved Oxford, showing her the chapel and library, stone gargoyles, perpendicular arches, rare volumes, and ornate Gothic carvings, explaining the age of every building and its historical and architectural significance. Joy exclaimed in delight over the pre-Raphaelite beauty of the stained-glass windows in St. Edmund Hall chapel.

"These are by William Morris and Edward Burne-Jones," Lewis told her, "and if you're not too tired I'll take you to see the Joshua Reynolds windows in New College chapel. Now those are truly magnificent; they represent the Seven Virtues and the Nativity. There's an El Greco painting in the chapel, too, of St. James. You really must see them."

"Next time," Joy begged off. "I am flagging a bit. Not as young as I once was."

"Oh, darling, am I wearing you out?" Lewis looked stricken.

"Don't be silly. I just don't want to use up all the goodies in one go." But she did appear to Jack to be weary, so he bundled Joy up and drove her home for tea at The Kilns.

On other occasions, they toured the greenhouses in the wonderful seventeenth century Botanic Gardens, then sat on lawn chairs, listening to an outdoor concert. They fed the swans in the Cherwell, noble birds who floated by majestically, like small royal yachts, and the ducks who scrabbled and squawked, jostling one another out of the way as they grabbed up the bread crusts Joy threw them. They watched the crews of eight rowing by in their swift shells. They packed picnic lunches into the Austin, and Warnie and Douglas came along for quiet afternoons, talking and reading on green grass under a bright blue August sky. Jack even taught Douglas to ride a bicycle, walking beside the wobbly wheels in a sun-drenched lane.

Autumn came, and with September the days grew noticeably shorter and cooler. Jack Lewis withdrew from his teaching schedule, at least "for the moment." The excursions came to an end, but Joy found ever-new enjoyment in The Kilns. Staying close to home was no hardship for either of them. She and Jack would walk slowly down the path to the pond and watch Douglas sail his paper boats. There would be tea served in the study, with Joy holding a kind of royal court from her bed.

If the days were shorter, the evenings were longer. They'd often sit in the drawing room and listen to plays and recitals on the wireless, and even rebroadcasts of Lewis's own talks. And they read books—Douglas and Joy shared one collection of books, while Joy and Jack shared another. They read aloud to one another; they played word games, they sang songs. Warnie taught Joy how to do the fiendish cryptic puzzles in the *Times,* and the two of them spent happy hours together tracking down the answers to the difficult clues.

In November, when a light snow was falling, Jack went up to London on the train, and returned from town loaded with parcels from Harrod's Food Hall. Among them was an amazing tin of jellied cranberry sauce, so that Douglas and Joy could have a really American Thanksgiving dinner. It was a very quiet dinner, because Joy was tired; she didn't say much, but Lewis could see by her pale face and dark-circled eyes that the pain was beginning to come back. He knew the time for them was growing as short as the wintry days. How was she to bear it? How were they both to bear it?

November slid too quickly into December. Joy seemed to disappear with the daylight. She kept more to her bed, moving only to a chair by the fire. She would pick a book up and try to read it, but it would fall from her fingers. Jack spent all his waking hours at her side, trying not to appear anxious. It was hard for Joy to talk, so Jack would read out loud to her while she lay with her eyes shut. Whether she heard him or not was hardly important; the only important thing was that he should remain by her side.

It was on a December evening, as they sat by the

fire, that the long moan escaped Joy's lips and she acknowledged her pain. The remission was officially over. As Lewis rose quickly from his chair and bent over her, searching her face, Joy looked into his eyes and whispered, "I'm sorry, Jack."

The ambulance arrived thirty minutes later to take Joy back to London and the hospital. Jack rode by her side all the way, clinging tightly to her hand. Once they arrived, attendants rushed the stretcher into X ray. Dr. Craig was already there, waiting for the films. As soon as they were ready, he mounted them on his light box and stared at them mutely, his face grim.

This time even Jack could understand the X rays. He could see the large dark masses covering his wife's cells; this was the cancer, spreading. The crab with its merciless pincers was attacking his beloved Joy and would not let go until it had taken her life. Cobalt radiation was no longer an option; all further treatments were useless.

"I'm so sorry, Mr. Lewis." Dr. Craig shook his head. It was out of his hands now, out of human hands entirely.

There was nothing more the doctors could do. It was only a matter of time now, and not much of that. Jack couldn't bear the thought of Joy lying alone in that hospital bed. The care she needed could be given to her at home. It was mostly a matter of morphine injections, and Joy trusted Jack to give them. There would be no more miracles; they'd used up their miracles. So, as the snow lay shining on Headington Hill, Joy Lewis came home to The Kilns again, this time to die.

After consultation with Warnie, who agreed, it was decided to turn the downstairs study into a bedroom for Joy. It was a cheerful room, with a fire that drew well, and a view over the garden. By moving things around, and sacrificing one of the comfortable chairs, they were able to bring a bed into the study. Warnie and Jack carried the bed down the stairs with some difficulty, but they managed to set it up close by the fire.

"She'll be better here," said Lewis quietly. "No stairs to climb." He couldn't begin to articulate the horror of the upstairs bedroom shorn of Joy's bed. An empty, soulless room now.

Douglas stood watching the moving activity, torn between dread and anger. "Can't you do something?"

If only he could tell the boy a lie! But he couldn't. Joy had seen to that. Joy had transformed Jack, made Jack completely honest. He shook his head. "I'm afraid not."

The boy stood stricken, tears welling in his eyes. Warnie's heart went out to him. "Tell you what,

Douglas. You couldn't go and fetch me the other pillow, could you?"

Douglas turned slowly and walked out of the room. He'd been spending a lot of his time the last couple of weeks in his favorite hiding place, the attic. He'd been rereading *The Magician's Nephew*, in which a small boy whose mother is very ill finds a magical fruit to make her well again. If Jack could invent the magic apple for a stranger, why couldn't he find one for Joy? Why does the magic have to end just when you really need it? Douglas couldn't understand why, but it made him very angry.

Douglas took a pillow from the bed in Jack's room, and went out again onto the landing. But he didn't go back downstairs; he couldn't. He wanted to be by himself. Clutching the pillow tightly to him, he stood looking out the window. The ambulance was just now driving up the hill; the boy could see it coming from where he was standing. It stopped at the gate, and the large back doors were opened. But this time it was not a smiling Joy in a wheelchair who came out into the spring sunshine. It was a still, silent figure on a stretcher, wrapped tightly in blankets against the icy winter afternoon. The boy watched as Jack, wearing his old sweater, came out to accompany the stretcher into the house.

It wasn't until later, when he was already in his pajamas with his teeth cleaned, that Douglas came into the study with Jack to see his mother. He was afraid to look, but Joy was sitting up in her bed, pillows propped behind her. Dr. Monk, who would be looking after her here at The Kilns, was packing up his medical bag.

"I'll be back tomorrow," said the doctor, and, to Douglas, "Good night, young man. Good night, Jack." This, in a lower tone, to his old friend, whom he could see was suffering nearly as much as Joy.

She was terribly thin and pale, but when she saw her son, Joy's drawn face lit up in a loving smile.

"A lot of silly fuss?" Joy said to the boy with the best smile she could manage.

Douglas nodded mutely.

"Get over here." The boy moved closer, and Joy took his hands in hers. Her hands were very cold although the fire was high and the room quite warm. "Give me a hug."

Climbing on the bed, Douglas threw himself into his mother's arms, and they kissed each other. The pain that his weight was causing her Joy kept hidden, but Jack could see it.

"Remember what we talked about," she said to Douglas with one last kiss. "Good night. Straight

247

to sleep." She watched him go, his back straight and his shoulder blades thin and sharp in the loose pajamas. Tears filled her eyes at the thought that she would never see him or know him as a man. *Be well, my son. Be happy.*

That evening, Jack kept vigil at his wife's side as she slept. Joy's sleep was not a peaceful one; when the pain returned, she cried out and opened her eyes. Jack leaped to his feet and bent over the bed to lift his suffering wife into his arms.

"God, I can't bear to see you in pain like this."

Joy tried to smile. "Keeps . . . me quiet."

"When it gets close, you find out whether you believe it or not."

The words came from Joy with great effort. "What is it . . . you always . . . say? 'Real . . . life hasn't . . . begun yet.' " She stopped as a fresh wave of pain swept over her. "Jack, you'd . . . better be . . . right."

Wordless now, they clung to each other, holding one another tightly to keep the dreaded moment at bay.

At least, Joy's eyes closed, and Lewis rose anxiously to bend over her. Was she still breathing? Yes, very faintly but regularly the blanket rose and fell over her bony form. With an explosive sigh of relief, Lewis sat down again in his chair and soon dozed off, sleeping fitfully and waking often. A couple of hours later, Joy opened her eyes and saw her husband watching her, fear and love in his eyes.

"Still . . . here?"

"Still here."

"Go to . . . bed. Get . . . some sleep."

"Soon."

She was very weak, and her voice was scarcely above a whisper. "Tell me . . . you'll be all . . . right."

"I'll be all right," he whispered back.

"Can . . . I . . . talk about . . . it?"

"Of course." Jack reached over and took her hand. It was terrifyingly cold.

"I'm . . . tired, Jack. I want . . . to rest. I just . . . don't want . . . to leave you."

"I don't want you to go." Tears started in Lewis's eyes.

Joy shut her eyes. "Too . . . much . . . pain."

"I know."

Her eyes opened again, and this time Jack saw a glow in them he didn't recognize. "I don't know what to do, Joy," he pleaded. "You'll have to tell me what to do."

Her grasp on his hand loosened. "You have to . . . let me go," she said simply.

"I'm not sure that I can," Jack wept.

She was too weak to say much more. Joy's eyes

fluttered shut, then opened immediately, fixing on
Jack. "Douglas . . . will you . . . take care . . . of
him for . . . me?"

"Of course," promised Jack.

"He . . . pretends not to . . . mind."

"I know."

"Like you."

"No more pretending, not anymore." Now Jack
Lewis was one of them, the numberless horde of
humanity that suffers unimaginable loss.

"I've . . . loved you so . . . much." Joy tried to
smile.

Her attempt at words were only weakening her.
"Don't talk, my love," he pleaded. "Just rest. My
love. Just rest."

Joy nodded faintly and closed her eyes. Weeping
openly, Jack stroked the dark hair away from Joy's
damp brow, and bent to kiss her cheek.

For several hours she didn't speak or move, but
Lewis could see that she was still breathing, although her breath was shallow. It wouldn't be long
now before her spirit would break free and go up
to God. Jack sat beside the bed, not counting the
minutes, but counting the breaths. After a while,
he just sat and stared into the darkness. At last,
he was moved to speak to her.

"I love you, Joy. I love you so much. You've made

me so happy. I didn't know I could be so happy. You're the truest person I've ever known.

"Sweet Jesus," he prayed, "be with my beloved wife Joy. Forgive me if I love her too much. Have mercy on us both."

Whether she heard his words to her or his prayers to God, Jack Lewis would never know. Joy didn't open her eyes and she didn't speak to him again. Yet she very well might have heard him, there was such a look of great peace on her face.

But very late in the night, at the time when the earth lies still and the salty tides go out, Joy Lewis let go of her life, of her final mortal agony. She died in silence, a silence that echoed through The Kilns.

In his small bed upstairs, Douglas Gresham woke up in terror at the exact moment of his mother's death. Young as he was, he understood the meaning of that profound silence. A few minutes later, Warnie Lewis woke up. He got out of bed and grabbed his dressing gown. Somehow, he, too, knew it was over, and he knew that there would be many things to do and that his brother would be needing him.

Jack Lewis sat slumped in the chair beside his wife's deathbed, his hands turned up helplessly in his lap, all hope, all love, drained from his face. It was over; Joy had left his life, and now he was alone.

On the day of Joy Lewis's funeral, Jack Lewis could not shed tears. He believed he had wept all the tears the world could hold, and now he was dry-eyed. Besides, what good did tears do? God never saw them; didn't listen to them any more than he listened to prayers. Only one black car followed the hearse with its flower-decked coffin, and in it sat Jack, Warnie, and Douglas, all of them stiff and silent. Each of the three sat solemn, lost in his own grief.

In *Mere Christianity*, C. S. Lewis had discussed Christian marriage at length, even though at that time he had never been married. He'd written with eloquence that the Christian marriage was based on Jesus Christ's teachings that husband and wife were of one flesh, a single organism, never to be divided unless by death. He'd understood those words with his fine theoretical mind, but never before had he truly understood them with his heart. He hadn't had the experience, you see. The experience that Joy always talked about, the experience that teaches everything worth knowing.

If he and Joy were truly one flesh, and Jack believed with all his heart that they were, then why hadn't he been allowed to share her pain?

Why hadn't he felt the agonies that racked her pathetic body. Why did God permit Jack Lewis to be bursting with good health and not permit him to share it with Joy?

How many times he'd told his enraptured audiences that God has a use for human pain! God the sculptor, man the stone. And pain made the sculpture perfect. Well, damn it, Jack Lewis didn't want to be perfect! He wanted Joy back, he wanted Joy alive and laughing and with him, in his arms. He no longer believed in his own words; they had left him hollow and empty and unable to weep.

Dry-eyed and stony-faced, Jack followed Joy's coffin to the Oxford crematorium chapel. It was a small service, attended only by Jack, Warnie, Douglas sitting in the front pew, Dr. Eddie Monk behind them, and in the back, Mrs. Young, openly sobbing into her handkerchief, sat next to the gardener Paxford, in his best suit, a rusty ancient affair, and a threadbare white shirt with a shiny detachable collar.

There were white flowers on the coffin, a shining sheaf of them, but no other floral tributes stood around the chapel. The organ played quietly, Bach. "Sheep May Safely Graze" and "Jesu, Joy of Man's Desiring," two of Joy's favorites. Warnie had arranged it, because Jack hadn't the strength to make arrangements.

Jack remained silent, sitting in the front pew. Lost in his grief, seeing and hearing almost nothing, he didn't even try to pray. Warnie noticed that Douglas didn't pray or cry, either. That was wrong; the boy should be able to weep tears for his mother. It was harmful to keep feelings like these locked up inside. Private grief like this was unhealthy. Warnie was worried about both of them.

The coffin was set down on rollers, which led like railway tracks to the crematorium behind the curtained doors. It was to Jack an obscenity, but cremation was what Joy had wanted, and he'd promised her. Now it didn't matter. What was left in the coffin wasn't Joy, anyway. It didn't have Joy's laughter, nor Joy's smiling dark gray eyes, nor Joy's mocking wit, nor Joy's reverent soul, nor Joy's loving heart. The coffin was only a box filled with cold clay.

The Reverend Harry Harrington conducted the simple service. "We therefore commit the body of thy servant Joy to the elements . . . earth to earth . . . ashes to ashes . . . dust to dust. . . ."

Oh, yes, thought Jack bitterly as the coffin rolled down the tracks through the curtained doors. In the sure and certain hope of the resurrection. That wonderful promised day. But suppose it never came? Suppose it was only a vain human hope for eternal life, a way of cheating death?

The service over, the handful of mourners filed out of the chapel. Warnie guided Douglas to the car; the boy was still dry-eyed. Lewis and Harrington were the last to leave. The chaplain felt he had to say something to his old friend, offer some word of comfort.

"Thank God for your faith, Jack. It's only faith that makes any sense of times like this. I know."

But Jack Lewis just turned his face silently to Harrington and looked at him with expressionless eyes. *He's empty*, thought the chaplain in shock, *Heaven help him, he's not the same man.*

With Joy's bed moved out of the study, it looked like the same old room again. Warnie had his old chair back, and Jack sat at his desk again. But he couldn't write, and didn't even go through his correspondence. Hundreds of letters of condolence had poured in from everywhere, but Jack had no interest in opening any of them. He just sat staring into the fire, at a loss for words or action. He kept his back deliberately turned to the engraving of the Golden Valley; he couldn't bear to see it, but he wasn't ready to take the picture down, either. Joy had loved it so much. Their place. Their own Golden Valley.

"What's happening to me, Warnie? I can't see

her anymore. I can't remember her face." He turned pleading eyes to his brother.

"I expect it's shock," answered Warnie with great sympathy.

Jack shuddered. "I'm so afraid. Of never seeing her again. Of thinking that suffering is just suffering after all. No cause. No purpose. No pattern. No sense. Just pain, in a world of pain."

"I don't know what to tell you, Jack," said Warnie painfully. It would take more eloquence than he possessed. Or, rather, it was likely that no amount of eloquence could reach his brother right now.

Jack shook his head slowly. "Nothing. There's nothing to say. I know that now. I've come up against a bit of experience, Warnie. Experience is a brutal teacher. But you learn, my God, you learn."

Joy's death from cancer was the talk of Magdalen College's senior common room. The dons discussed it over their evening sherries. There appeared to be a mild disagreement about whether or not any or all of them should have attended Joy's funeral. In any event, the talk was academic, because the funeral was over, and none of them had gone.

"I wouldn't say this to Jack," remarked the

Reverend Harry Harrington in a solemn tone, "but in the circumstances better sooner than later."

"Is he taking it very hard?" asked Rupert Parrish.

"I'm afraid so," sighed the chaplain.

At that moment, much to their surprise, Jack Lewis himself came in, accompanied by his brother Warnie. An awkward silence greeted them, as the dons tried to think of something to say.

"Evening, Jack," Riley called out with false heartiness.

"I wasn't going to come," said Lewis. "Then I thought I would."

Harrington thought it was up to him as a man of the cloth to say something consoling. "Life must go on."

Jack's stony expression didn't change. "I don't know that it must, Harry. But it certainly does."

Warnie poured two glasses of sherry and handed one to his brother.

"I'm sorry, Jack," said Christopher Riley sincerely. He hated to see his old friend like this, like an empty shell of a man.

"Thank you, Christopher."

"We're all sorry, Jack."

"Thank you, President."

"Anything I can do?" Riley asked.

"Just don't tell me it's all for the best, that's all."

"Only God knows why these things have to happen," said Harry Harrington.

"God knows? But does God care?"

"We see so little, Jack. We're not the Creator—"

Suddenly, without warning, the dam broke and Jack Lewis's fury broke forth. "No, we're the creatures, aren't we? We're the rats in the cosmic laboratory. I've no doubt the experiment is for our own good, but that still makes God the vivisectionist, doesn't it?"

Jack Lewis's grief was bitter and his anger with God a storm that shook him. He was sick to death of pieties, mouthed without understanding. He hated himself for having been one of them, one of those who thought he had all the answers. He had no answers; perhaps there were no answers. Most likely God was looking down right now—if He ever did bother to look down—and was laughing at the puny show of human sorrow.

"Jack—" the chaplain put a hand out to touch his friend on the arm, but Lewis wrenched his arm away savagely. His face was distorted by rage, and his eyes were blazing like rocket fire. "No, Harry, it won't do! This is a bloody awful mess, and that's all there is to it!"

Jack broke off suddenly, as though recalling himself, and, giving himself a little shake, he put his sherry glass down on a table. "I'm sorry. I shouldn't have come. I'm not fit company." Lewis turned and walked out of the room, with Warnie hurrying after him, leaving an uncomfortable silence in his wake.

They started home together up Headington Hill, saying nothing for the first half-mile.

"Jack," began Warnie.

"Yes."

"Your grief is your own business. Maybe you feel that life is a mess. Maybe it is. But there's Douglas."

"Douglas?" The name felt strange on Jack's tongue. "What about Douglas?"

"Talk to him."

"I don't know what to say to him," cried Jack in despair.

But Warnie, kind, stolid, sympathetic, unchangeable Warnie, lost his temper with his brother. Warnie, who never raised his voice, now raised his voice. "Just *talk* to him!"

Lewis knew where to look for Douglas first, and that's where he found him, in the attic. But the boy wasn't curled up in his usual chair reading, he was sitting on the floor in a total attitude of dejection, his legs drawn up and his arms wrapped around them, while his chin rested on his knees. Douglas was staring into space, but seeing, Jack knew, nothing.

"Hi," said Jack softly, and Douglas answered "Hi." With a sigh, Lewis lowered himself to the attic floor to sit beside Douglas, unconsciously adopting the same posture. For a moment or two they sat in silence, side by side, then Jack Lewis spoke again.

"Douglas, when my mother died I was your age. I thought that if I prayed for her to get better, and if I really believed she'd get better, then she wouldn't die. But she did."

"It doesn't work," said Douglas sadly.

"No," confessed Lewis. "It doesn't work."

"I don't care," said the boy, meaning that he cared with all his heart.

"I loved your mother very much. Perhaps I loved her too much. She knew that. She said to me, is it worth it? She knew what it would be like later. It doesn't seem fair, does it?"

"I don't see why she had to get sick," the boy said in a muffled whimper.

"No, nor I. But you can't hold on to things, Douglas. You have to let them go."

"Jack?"

"Yes."

"Do you believe in Heaven?"

There followed a long pause. "Yes, I do," Lewis said finally, because, despite everything, he still did. He still clung to the resurrection into eternal bliss.

"I don't believe in Heaven," Douglas said sadly.

"That's okay." Okay. That had been Joy's word. Douglas's word. An American word. When had Jack begun to use it? He didn't know.

"I sure would like to see her again."

"Me, too."

This boy was all that was left to Jack of Joy. He was her legacy to him; he even had some of her features, and her honesty. Jack Lewis put his arm around Douglas, and the boy turned and buried his head in the man's shoulder. The tears, so long withheld, finally came freely, cleansing their pain-filled hearts. Together, holding each other tightly on the floor of the old attic, they wept.

Slowly, slowly, things began to return to normal. Not to where they were before Jack had met Joy—that could never be the same again. But work helped; work and family were the only things that did help. Warnie was, as always, a rock, and Douglas had been folded into their family like a son to both brothers. C. S. Lewis began writing again, and took up his seminar and tutorial schedule.

Lewis was approaching his study rooms at Magdalen College and was about to enter when he saw a serious-faced young man waiting. The boy cleared his throat; evidently he had been waiting for Professor Lewis. "Who are you?" asked Jack.

"Chadwick, sir. You're my tutor this term."

"Am I? You'd better come in, then, hadn't you?"

Together, they climbed the stairs to Lewis's study. The boy stood nervously until Jack gestured him to a seat. Then he picked up his old pipe, perched on the corner of his desk, and watched the boy while he filled the pipe from his tobacco tin. "Chadwick, you say?"

"Yes, sir."

"Sit down."

Lewis lit up his pipe and took a long puff of the smoke. "We read to know we're not alone." He looked sharply at the undergraduate. "Do you think that is so?"

"I hadn't thought of it like that before, sir." The boy's dark eyes held a familiar awe. He was actually being questioned by the legendary C. S. Lewis.

"No. Nor had I," said Lewis quietly. "I suppose some people would say we *love* to know we're not alone. Would you?"

The young man began to speak, hesitantly at first, then with increasing confidence. "Well, if you mean falling in love, well I haven't, really. I probably know more about love from books than from personal experience." *So did I,* thought

Lewis. *So did I, for so many years. How much I had to learn! How much I did learn, thanks to Joy, my teacher, my love.* He didn't know whether to envy this young man for the experience that still lay before him, or to pity him for the pain he would have to endure. On the whole, envy, he supposed. Yes, surely, envy, for the experience of love that waited somewhere for young Chadwick.

"Go on, I'm listening," Lewis encouraged the student. He went to the window of his study, which was usually kept shut. He threw it open and leaned out, feeling the coolness of fresh air on his face, smelling the air, the grass below. Behind him, his student continued to talk.

"Why love, if losing hurts so much? I have no answers anymore, only the life I've lived. Twice in that life I've been given the choice, as a boy, and as a man. The boy chose safety. The man chooses suffering. The pain, now, is part of the happiness, then. That's the deal."

Jack Lewis put his pen down and smiled, thinking of Joy. He wished he could read her these words, but never mind. Jack had a feeling she had heard them; she was never far away from him now.